RIP TIDE
BIKINI

Lyla Dune

RIP TIDE BIKINI
A Pleasure Island Romance

http://www.lyladune.com

ComposeSum@gmail.com

This book is a work of fiction. Names, characters, places and incidents are either a product of the author's imagination, fictitious or used fictitiously. Any resemblance to actual persons living or dead, business establishments, or locales is entirely coincidental.

Cover art from Jupiter Images/ Getty Images
Photography by John Smith/Corbis
Copyright © 2014 Composesum Publishing LLC

Mama, you left this world much too soon. I wish we would have had more time together. I know you're watching over me as my guardian angel.

This book is for you, Mama.

Table of Contents

CHAPTER ONE
Chase

Earl the Squirrel was nuts!

Trent McAllister skidded to a halt in his SUV, as the drawbridge traffic arm came down right in front of him. On a red hot Harley, Earl Washington zoomed up the Pleasure Island bridge mid-rise.

Holy shit! He's going for it.

Trent tightened his grip on the steering wheel and held his breath as Earl sailed through the air on his motorcycle. When the lunatic landed safely on the other side of the bridge, after having crossed a gap of at least fifteen feet, Trent released a shuddering breath. He wanted to bring the guy in. But he didn't want to be responsible for the raging idiot killing himself.

Fugitive recovery was Trent's job. He'd been called the best and fastest runner in the Carolinas. Technically, bounty hunting was illegal in North Carolina, that's why they used the term "runner", but the average person still called it bounty hunting, nonetheless.

Trent had been chasing Earl for the past two weeks. Two long, exhausting weeks.

The chase had gotten real old, real fast. Normally, he would've had his guy in a day or two at the most. The more criminals he could bring in, the more money he made. This slippery thief was the biggest challenge he'd ever had. And it had stopped being fun a week ago, when Trent lost his ranking to his nemesis Stan Harris. All because of Squirrel.

Trent dropped his head to the steering wheel and closed his eyes. He could hardly believe he was actually relieved Earl had survived the reckless stunt unscathed, but he was. From the information he'd gathered on the guy, Earl wasn't all bad. Just got mixed in with a lowlife crowd and was running scared. But the law was the law. It wasn't Trent's job to play judge and jury. Guilty or not guilty would be decided in the courtroom. Trent was simply making sure the young man showed up in court. That's all.

There was no need to get personal about cases. That's one of the reason Trent liked the job. No getting personal. Personal always led to trouble. And once things got personal, they usually left more than one person hurt.

He'd had enough pain. Divorce on the heels of medical discharge nearly did him in. After all that training to become a Navy SEAL, he only got to serve four years of active duty, and only three months in the same house with his ex, not that he was convinced more time together would have changed the outcome.

Yep, it was official: He'd turned thirty, and his life had turned to shit.

On top of his hardships and shortcomings, now he was forced to add slow and soft to his list of undesirable attributes, two labels a man couldn't wear with pride.

He needed to excel at something, have a purpose, otherwise, why was he here? Why had he survived when six of his seven teammates had perished? If it hadn't been for the quick thinking of Conrad Mitchell, he wouldn't be alive today. Luckily, Conrad hadn't endured any serious injury and remained on active duty, while Trent did all he could to simply remain active. Because whenever he stopped for any length of time, the violent memories and the unshakable loss of everything dear to him, including his sense of self worth, caused him to spiral into depression.

He needed a mission, which is something being a runner gave him. And he strived to be the best. That's why Jimmy, the bail bondsman he worked with, called him first whenever big money was involved.

Trent was "the man".'Til that scrawny Earl caused him to lose his title. Now, Stan was the man. Stan the man? Jesus.

The more he thought about it, the madder he got. He

knew Pleasure Island was Earl's hometown and that his sister Mazy lived there. When the bridge lowered, Trent stomped on the gas. He had a slippery squirrel to catch.

A motorcycle sped down the driveway, and Mazy Washington rolled out from under the jeep she was working on. Her brother roared into the garage and ground to a stop mere inches from here head. The smell of burning rubber filled the air. "Earl! Damn!"

He climbed off the bike. "Holy hell, I didn't see you there. Sorry, sis."

"What's the deal?" Mazy hadn't seen Earl in months, and here he was plowing into the garage, wild-eyed and hassling for breath. She pushed to her feet.

"Got a bounty hunter on my ass. That's the deal." He paced, hands on hips, cursing under his breath.

"I thought you cleaned up your act. You promised. What did you do now?" Mazy's heart went into her throat. Earl had gotten mixed up with the wrong crowd during their senior year of high school, right after their mother died. He'd dropped out of school and joined a roughneck group of thieves who broke into rich vacation homes on the island while the owners were away. When Earl landed himself in jail, it had torn her apart. Their dad stayed on the road, biking with his buddies, attempting to escape the grief of their mom's death. He didn't even bother to come home when Earl got in trouble. Mazy stayed put in the trailer she grew up in and tried to make a life for herself. She was determined to make good on the promise she'd made her mother to keep this family together by making sure the guys had a place to call home.

Earl removed his helmet, his curly red hair soaking wet and plastered to his head. "I did clean up my act. I've been installing duct, crawling under houses, climbing into hot attics. I ain't done nothing illegal."

Earl was a pot head. She gave him a smirk. "*Nothing illegal?*"

"Nothing! I have to take the piss test for work."

His eyes were clear, and he held her gaze without wavering. If he'd been lying, he would have looked away. She knew how to read him. He was telling the truth.

"Mazy, you gotta believe me. I didn't do it this time. I swear. Some thugs are trying to pin me for larceny, and I think they're gonna try to frame me for murder too, at least that's what my buddy said."

"Murder?" Damn, that made her dizzy. She put her hand on the hood of the jeep to steady herself. "What the hell, Earl?"

"I didn't do it." He grasped her arm, his face dialed to *Help Me.*

She sucked in a deep breath and blinked away the blurriness until she could focus again. "I know. You'd never kill anybody. Tell me everything."

"No time. You gotta trust me. This bounty has been sticking to me like glue. I ain't never had this much trouble losing a tail."

Earl's terror was contagious. They had that twin connection. Whatever was going on, he needed her help. And she wasn't going to let him down.

She noticed he was in jeans and a white tank just like she was. They both had the same tat on their right bicep in honor of their mother. Earl was skinny and so was she. They both had curly red hair. She wore her hair short for years, but had recently let it grow out. Today, she hadn't straightened it, and it was pulled into a ponytail.

She said, "Give me your vest and helmet."

He handed them over. "What you got in mind?"

"I'm gonna lose your tail for you."

"You think you can do it?"

Earl would never admit it, but Mazy had always handled a bike better than he had. Sometimes she'd let him outrun her so his ego wouldn't be bruised in front of his friends. But she knew he was well aware she could ride circles around him.

"I know I can. Take the VW sitting out back. I got it running great. It's gassed up. Keys are on the pegboard. Peace sign keychain."

"Thanks, sis."

She hopped on his bike, tugged the helmet in place and freed a few curls at the base of her neck. "Call me as soon as you can." The last time he'd called her, he was heading to Mexico and using a disposable phone. Hopefully, he'd bought a new one.

"I will. Listen, don't try pulling no crazy stuff, just lead him around the island long enough for me to get out of here." He passed her his damp vest that reeked of perspiration and gasoline.

She slid it on and cringed. This was love—wearing someone else's stinky, sweaty denim vest. She caught Earl's concerned gaze with hers and gave him her best reassuring smile. "I got this."

The creases in his brow relaxed, and he blew out a breath. "I mean it, Mazy. I don't want you getting hurt. This guy is relentless. He's been chasing me down for two weeks, and he don't let up. He's got balls of steel."

She envisioned those desktop clacker balls. Probably not what her brother had in mind. Earl straightened the collar on the vest. The look on his face made her chest tighten. His eyes said, "I love you." They weren't a mushy family. She and Earl *never* said they loved each other, but that didn't mean they didn't feel it.

She nodded.

Earl lifted his chin. "I'll call ya as soon as I can." His voice was hoarse and emotional.

Damn it. A lump swelled in her throat. "You better."

Mazy pulled out of the garage then spun out of the driveway onto the dead end road that led to her trailer. A black SUV with a white top barreled toward her. That had to be the bounty hunter. She darted across the street and took the dirt path that led to the ostrich farm. She knew the hunter would follow. He didn't know this island like she did. This was going to be a piece of cake.

Trent McAllister leaned forward when Earl's Harley peeled out from his sister's driveway. The redheaded, scrawny S.O.B. went off road. That was fine by Trent. His FJ could handle it.

Trent knuckled down and followed suit, zipping between the pines, keeping Earl in his sights.

Squirrel made a hard left and disappeared behind a shed. Damn it. The dirt path was well worn. There were so many tracks in the sand it was hard to tell which were Earl's. Trent spotted fresh tread marks, single file. They led to an opened gate.

In the expansive field beyond the gate, a dust cloud moved across the sand at top speed.

Sure enough, a red motorcycle was leading the cloud.

"I gotcha now, Squirrel."

Earl whipped around sideways, came to a stop, and whistled like he was calling a dog. Popping a wheelie, he continued toward a bright fuchsia house perched on a hill.

Trent drove through the gate into a patch of tall dry grass. Movement to his right got his attention. Five, monolithic birds sprinted toward him. Were those ostriches?

Struggling to not let the prehistoric-looking creatures distract him, he squinted and made out a flash of red on the other side of the field.

He kept driving, bumping over the rough terrain.

An ostrich ran in front of the SUV. Trent slammed on brakes to keep from hitting the big ass bird. That thing was HUGE. My God. They didn't look so monstrous in pictures.

He was so busy gawking at Godzilla with feathers that he lost sight of Earl. *This wasn't happening.*

Swerving to the right, he dodged the flock of ostriches. When he got to where he'd last seen Earl's dust cloud, he spotted a single track going off to the right.

He turned, and his front tires left the ground as he hit a bump. Next thing he knew, his whole front end slammed down into a ditch, and his airbags inflated.

Because of the grass, he hadn't seen that coming. *Airbag in face...Can't breathe....*

He fought with the airbag until he could see out of his windshield.

Where did that Squirrel go?

Was that dust or smoke billowing out from the front of his vehicle?

He sniffed. Smoke. *Sweet mother.*

He flinched in horror. Orange flames licked his front bumper. Fire. *You gotta be kidding me.*

The hot engine must have ignited the dry grass.

He wrestled and punched the airbag out of his way and pulled himself out of the SUV. Flames and gasoline were not something to hang around. He quickly moved to a safe distance from the rapidly growing fire before remembering he had important paperwork on Earl in the vehicle. For a split second, the urge to retrieve the documents tempted him, but Earl wasn't worth risking his own life over. He had most of Earl's information memorized anyway.

Car insurance probably wouldn't cover the fire. Chances were, Trent would be charged with reckless driving, at the very least. But none of that hurt nearly as bad as watching his brand new SUV go up in flames. He still owed a hefty hunk of change on that ride.

The heat pouring off the vehicle intensified and Trent took a few blind steps backward. Something hard whacked him in the back of the skull. *What the*? He spun around in time to see a bird bill heading straight for his face. His hands came up in defense. An ostrich pecked his palm, causing Trent to punch himself in the eye.

Ostrich wings unfurled and cast a shadow over him. Trent ducked, but didn't successfully avoid another peck from the giant bird. This time the feathered beast nailed him good, right between the eyes, causing him to fall backward. Kicking up at the lunging ostrich, he heard himself scream like a girl as he rolled out of the way and scrambled to his feet.

He sprinted toward the gate on the other side of the field, as if the flames from his SUV had lit his ass on fire. Glancing back, the bird was inches away. The dang thing ran FAST! One of its large talons kicked him in the back of the leg and Trent went down.

A loud explosion shook the earth. There went the SUV.

He looked up at the bird from hell with a tuft of black feathers standing straight up on the middle of its head like a Mohawk. "Oh, God! This is it. I'm a dead man."

A strange whistle sounded and a man's voice called out, "Spike! You stop that! Git!"

The ostrich went still and looked in the direction of the voice.

With a quiet cluck, the bird sauntered away calmly.

Trent wiped blood and sweat out of his eyes, blinking.

A thin old man in overalls and a plaid shirt crawled off a

green tractor and walked toward him. "You okay?"

Multiple sirens sounded in the distance, fire department, police, and ambulance.

"I will be." He sat up.

The old man waved smoke out of his face and surveyed the property. "I wish I could say the same for my farm. Mind telling me why you're trespassing?"

Oh shit. Trespassing, starting a fire, reckless driving, the charges were piling up fast. He'd be the laughing stock of his home county when they got wind of this.

Flashing red and blue lights flickered through the pines. "I didn't realize I was trespassing. The gate was wide open."

The old man gave him a disgusted look. "I suppose if I leave my back door open, that means you're welcome to waltz right in?"

"No, of course not." Trent jumped to his feet, and a wave of dizziness overcame him. He placed a hand on his head. There was a huge lump forming on his forehead.

"Hold tight, son. The ambulance is on its way."

Trent's vision blurred, then everything went black.

Mazy rolled Earl's motorcycle into Louise Moore's garage. She glanced at her watch. Three o'clock. Louise would most likely be hanging out with her friends on the beach. Mazy winced at the thought of trying to find her in the crowd of naked seniors parading around Bare Point, but she needed to talk to her. There was no better way to get word around the island than to tell Louise Moore or Myrtle Pinkerton a juicy tidbit. Wherever Louise was, Myrtle was never far away.

Louise's voice drifted through the air. "Fire department's on the way. You get ahold of Carl?"

"Yep." Mazy would recognize that crackling high-pitched

voice anywhere. Myrtle Pinkerton. Myrtle continued. "He's headed to the north end of the farm now. Said he'd already seen the smoke." Myrtle grunted and groaned. "No fair, you've hogged them thangs long enough. Let me have a look!"

Good Lord. What were these two women up to?

"Hang on, you ole hussy." Louise ground out then whistled like a construction worker ogling a pretty girl. "My oh my! He's fodder for wet-dreams."

"Let me see, damn you!" Myrtle was in a serious huff. Mazy had never heard her cuss Louise out like that.

When Mazy reached the top of the stairs that led to Louise's deck, there stood Louise and Myrtle, side by side, butt-naked, and they were fighting over a pair of binoculars. Louise's tall, pudgy frame towered over tiny Myrtle.

Louise had to be 5'10" at least. Her hair resembled Bozo the clown's, a shade of red not found in nature, or at least not on humans. Myrtle made a habit of teasing her about it, saying her hair was menopausal red, 'cause only menopausal women ever chose that particular hue. Mazy suspected Louise's menopausal days had ended long ago, but she'd never point that out.

Myrtle was thin and under five feet tall. Her hair wasn't much better than Louise's though. It was fuzzy, light blue like dryer lint after a load of blue jeans.

Little Miss Fuzzy Head looked up at Ronald McDonald's granny, who was gazing through the binoculars with a wicked grin on her face. Myrtle jabbed a finger into her friend's belly button like she thought she was kin to The Pillsbury Doughboy and made Louise lean forward and grab her tummy.

Myrtle popped to her tiptoes and snagged the binoculars away with a giggle, then held them up to her eyes. "Oh my word, yes. He's a looker. If that ostrich don't kill him, we're gonna have fun with this one. Ouch. That had to hurt. Poor baby, Myrtle will kiss it and make it better. Don't you worry." She looked up at Louise and smiled. "He sure has a nice ass, don't he?"

Mazy couldn't help but look in the direction the ladies were gazing. Smoke? Great day. Had the bounty hunter caught the field on fire? "Good Lord!" She squinted to make out more details.

"Hey, Mazy. Come on up for a look. The fire's nothing to be too worried about. Too much sand for it to spread. We already called the fire department. You gotta see this hot man being chased by one of Carl's ostriches." Louise's voice was filled with amusement.

Myrtle covered her mouth and snickered. "He thinks he can outrun it. He ain't local, that's for sure. Everybody 'round here knows you can't outrun an ostrich. Ooo boy, but he sure is trying. We ought to give him a gold medal for fastest sprint." She lowered the binoculars and batted her eyes, as if she were having trouble refocusing, then made eye contact with Mazy. "You know him?"

Mazy shook her head. "I haven't met him. Well, not exactly. I kinda led him into the field, though."

"What did you do that for? Carl don't like people driving through the farm." Myrtle scowled.

"I know, and I had no idea the jerk would start a fire. How he managed to do that is beyond me."

Louise took a step toward Mazy and motioned her to come closer. "You look like you got something serious on your mind."

These two old women had a knack for reading Mazy, always had. Seemed they had some kind of sixth sense about things. Earl jokingly said they were witches with the power to read minds. The power to get people to confess all was more like it. Since childhood, Mazy had laid her problems at the feet of these two women. They were like family to her. She didn't have any living grandmothers, but she had Louise and Myrtle, and she was glad of it. After her mother passed away, she needed them more than ever.

They'd offered comfort and guidance to Earl too, and they'd want to know what was going on with him.

"Y'all, Earl is in trouble again. Big trouble. That guy in the field is a bounty hunter." Mazy's hands began to shake. She still hadn't come to terms with the idea of Earl in hot water with the law again, much less being labeled a killer. "Somebody framed him for larceny, and word has it they're trying to frame him for murder. He jumped bail."

Louise gasped. "Murder? That's a load of bullshit. Earl may not be the brightest star in the sky, and he may have gotten himself mixed up with some scoundrels back in the day, but he wouldn't hurt a soul."

Myrtle sat the binoculars down on a nearby table. "Who in their right mind would even fall for such a lie? Hell, you don't have spend more than ten minutes with the boy to know he ain't the kind to take a life. You just tell us how we can help."

Mazy walked over to the table and picked up the binoculars. She zoomed in on the bounty hunter. His head was bleeding and the ostrich looked like it was about to go in for a lethal peck. "Oh God. I didn't want him dead."

"Who? The bounty hunter?" Louise asked.

"Don't fret. Here comes Carl. He'll settle that bully bird down." Myrtle seemed confident.

Mazy hoped she was right. Whew. She was. The bird walked off.

Mazy gave the ladies her most pitiful look. "We need to stall this guy as long as possible so Earl can put some distance between them. I was hoping y'all would spread the word. If we work together, I'm pretty sure we can think of ways to keep him here for a while."

"I wouldn't mind seeing him hang around. He's mighty fine." Myrtle waggled her eyebrows. "Consider it done."

Mazy peered into the binoculars just in time to see the SUV blow sky high. Her mouth fell open.

"He ain't going nowhere anytime soon, now." Louise laughed.

Myrtle slapped her thigh. "I'd say your problem just solved itself. I'll get ahold of Carl and see what we can do to detain this fella for a while."

A fire truck, a couple of police cars, and an ambulance drove onto the field. Luckily, the blazing grassy area was surrounded by bald patches of sand, and the fire hadn't spread too far. Nowhere near the woods. It'd be easy to put out.

Mazy couldn't help but feel relieved the ambulance had arrived. The bounty hunter had taken quite a hit on the head. The back of his collar was stained with blood, not to mention his face. The poor man looked like he'd endured a serious butt-kicking, and she felt responsible. She was one part proud, one part ashamed, and one big part relieved he wasn't going to catch Earl anytime soon.

She had to admit Myrtle was right, though. That bounty hunter did have a fine ass. Mighty fine.

CHAPTER TWO
Snoop

A medic with Luke on his nametag gave Trent a serious look. "Sure you don't want to let us take you to the hospital so the doctor can have a look at you?"

Trent waved the medic, Luke, away and stood. "I'm positive. Just overheated and dehydrated. Much better now." The hospital was the last place he wanted to go. He'd spent enough time being pricked and probed to last a lifetime. Just the thought of stepping foot inside a waiting room made him tense. Besides, he knew what a brain injury felt like, and this peck on back of the head may have drawn a little blood, but it was far from anything to be concerned about. Plus, it'd already started scabbing over. An ice pack for his eye. Plenty of water in his system. He'd be fine.

The medic's assessing gaze appeared unconvinced. The young man's mouth twisted as if he was unsure what to say. With raised eyebrows, he looked over at the farmer who shrugged and said, "It's up to him. Don't look at me."

Returning his attention back to Trent, Luke frowned and said, "Okay then. If you change your mind, give us a call."

Trent nodded. "I'm good. Really. Thanks for everything."

The farmer was talking to two policemen, and Trent's stomach churned. The old man patted one of the officers on the shoulder then walked toward Trent. Here it comes.

Standing less than a foot away from him, the farmer put his hands in his front pockets and held Trent's gaze. "My farmhand went on vacation. I thought I could handle things by myself with no trouble for a couple of weeks, but as it turns out, I'm having a time of it."

Trent just stared at him, wondering what that had to do with him.

The old man took off his straw hat and smoothed a few gray stands across his ruddy, balding scalp. "What you say you stick around for a spell, help me on the farm, and I forget about the trespassing, the fire, the property damage?" Cocking his head, the farmer's lips curled slightly, as if he found humor in the situation.

Crazy old man. Who makes offers like that? Maybe he could buy the guy off instead of hanging around.

Trent looked deep into the codger's eyes, trying to get a read on his character. Trent was usually an excellent judge of character, always had been. The skill came in handy through the years too. But he didn't always follow his gut. Every time he'd ignored his instincts, he'd come to regret it.

His instincts were telling him this farmer was an upstanding guy who could be trusted. More than that, his gut was telling him that helping the old man was the least he could do. Trent would be a real asshole to turn him down.

The SUV was a heap of burnt junk now. Earl was long gone too. Not a doubt in his mind. He might as well give up the ghost on this one. He was going to be stuck here a day or two anyway. It'd take that long to sort things out and get his buddy to bring him his motorcycle.

Burn a man's field then walk away without helping him clean it up? Nah. That didn't feel right at all.

Besides, Trent hadn't stayed put anywhere since his divorce. He'd kept moving, focused on the task at hand so he didn't have to look back, so the memories couldn't tackle him for good. Maybe if the farmer kept him busy, he could handle it. Maybe.

Trent nodded to the old guy. "I don't know anything about farming and even less about ostriches."

"No real farming involved. Not growing any crops here. Just some livestock to feed. Nothing too hard about that." A grin curled at the corners of the old man's mouth.

Something about him reminded Trent of his grandfather who'd passed away years ago. The best times from Trent's childhood were spent fishing and hanging out with his grandfather. "You got yourself a deal...Mr?"

"Carl's the name."

"All right, Carl. Not like I'm in the position to go anywhere right now anyway. I'd be happy to lend a hand." When he said it, he was surprised how much he meant it. Why? Maybe because ever since he'd been discharged he'd felt more lost than ever and something about getting back to a simpler way of life felt right. "I'm Trent McAllister. You got yourself a farmhand." He offered his hand. Carl's firm handshake was solid, honest. You can tell a lot about a man by his handshake, and Trent could tell he and Carl were gonna get along just fine.

The kind gentleman let go of Trent's hand and took a step back. "I got a guest house. If you need a place to stay, you're welcome to it."

"Sounds good to me." Free room? Too good to pass up.

Carl gestured Trent over to his tractor. "Hop on and I'll give ya the tour."

Mazy laughed. "I'm serious as a heart attack, Earl. Days. Not sure exactly how many, but at least two. Reckon that's enough time for you to do whatcha gotta do?"

"Hell, I hope so. I wasn't expecting this. I thought a couple hours head start would be a blessing, but I ain't gonna lie, knowing you got him tied up, and I don't have to look over my shoulder every second is sure gonna make my life easier. I might actually get some sleep tonight. A shower, good food, soft bed. Man, that'll be nice." The relief in Earl's voice made Mazy smile. "Listen, sis, I wanna get on down the road while I still got some daylight. I'll call you in the morning."

"Sure thing. You be careful. Talk in the morning."

Whew. Earl could breathe and so could she.

A shower did sound good. After that romp through the dusty field, she was covered in dirt, and her jeans were stuck to her sweaty body.

She peeled off her clothes and jumped in the shower. Cool water, floral scented body wash, loofa pad. Ahh. Dark, sudsy streams rolled off of her and swirled down the drain.

Trent took in the quaint cottage with its small kitchen, sitting area, and master bedroom sparsely decorated, yet homey, and said, "This is just fine, Carl. Thanks for putting me up."

The farmer pointed toward the bedroom with an antique brass bed covered by a quilt of pastel hues. "I think there's some clothes that'll fit ya in the closet. Help yourself to whatever you need. My girlfriend, Myrtle, keeps the place pretty well stocked with necessities, but if you find you need something, just give me a call. My number's at the top of a phone list on the fridge." He took a few steps back and reached toward the mantle and adjusted a picture of a lanky teen boy and what looked like a much younger Carl standing on a pier holding an enormous fish between them, both guys smiling. "I imagine you're tuckered out after the ordeal you went through. I'm glad Spike didn't do any permanent damage."

"Nah. He tagged me pretty hard in the back of the head, but barely broke the skin. The EMT cleaned it up and put antibacterial salve on it. Said it wasn't much of a cut, more of an abrasion. I'm sure it looked worse than it was. Head injuries bleed easily. The black-eye's from my own damn fist. That's the funny part." Trent offered the old man a smile, hoping to reassure him.

"Well, you just keep using that ice pack to manage the swelling. Seems to be doing the trick. You're eye's not nearly as puffy anymore."

"Will do."

The farmer patted Trent's shoulder. "Get some rest. We can go over the chore stuff in the morning."

"Sounds good. Thanks again."

As soon as the old man left, Trent took a quick shower and rifled through the oak dresser in the bedroom until he'd found a pair of khaki cargo shorts and a blue surfer T-shirt. The shirt fit snugly across Trent's chest and arms. The shorts were a tad baggy, but they'd do for now. He opted to go commando. No way was he wearing another man's drawers.

He put his tennis shoes back on and walked out of the cottage and across the farm that was about the size of four football fields combined. A tall fence made from chicken wire surrounded the ostrich infested land mass. Smoke, or rather the stench of it, lingered in the air. As he reached the blackened grass, he was pleasantly surprised by how little of the field had been damaged. At the time, he'd thought he'd caused a raging inferno, but judging from the contained ashen area, it hadn't been half as bad as he remembered. The ground had already soaked up most of the water the firemen had sprayed onto the flames.

Crunching over the burnt stalks of grass, he lumbered toward what was left of his vehicle and poked around in the pile of twisted metal and melted synthetics that reminded him of the bombed jeeps from his last mission. He closed his eyes, pushing back haunting images of war. Images of his buddies, their mangled bodies, and the sounds of their cries in agony.

His stomach lurched, and his hands began to sweat.

He'd never be able to scrub those horrific details from his mind, and they seemed to have a way of pushing to the forefront of his thoughts at the slightest trigger.

Do NOT let yourself go there. Don't.

Focus. Is there anything in this rubble worth saving?

He kicked at what appeared to be the remains of the driver's seat. Atop a pile of ash sat half of a warped steering wheel. Useless. The SUV was charred and in a million pieces scattered about. Some of the debris had been flung twenty feet, at least.

That damn Squirrel.

Last he'd seen Earl Washington, he'd been heading toward a big fuchsia house on the hill. Trent shielded his eyes from the late afternoon sun and gazed up at the colorful house. *Wonder who lives there? Some of Earl's relatives?*

Turning his back on the mysterious beach cottage, Trent meandered toward the woods and the gate he'd entered earlier. He followed his old tracks around the shed and down a dirt path, until he reached the road. On the other side of the two-lane street was Earl's sister's place.

Next thing he knew, he was sneaking onto her property. He didn't have permission to be snooping about, but he couldn't help himself. He had a better chance of sniffing out leads while it was still light out and before the trail went cold.

A driveway of gravel and oyster shells led to an old, aqua and white, single-wide mobile home sitting a good seventy feet from the road. A dozen or so dilapidated vehicles and at least two dozen rusty lawnmowers were parked in an open area beside a huge detached garage clad in beige vinyl siding that made the house trailer seem dinky in comparison. A hand-painted sign hung over the wide garage door. "The Pits – Open when the sun is shining and the hearse is out front." He chuckled. Hearse? Sure enough a few feet to the left of the garage was a purple hearse. License plate: DAPITS.

The air was humid and thick with the scent of pine. He wove his way through the trees, creeping quietly over pine straw, slowly stepping around brittle looking limbs and pine cones. As he neared the trailer, he heard the sound of drums.

Drumbeats vibrated the ground and seemed to cause the dogwood leaves to dance. The woods were alive with sound. Intricate rhythms reminiscent of tribal festivals around camp fires caused the energy in the air to shift and make him all the more curious. He hid behind a large oak with Spanish moss dripping from its branches.

Azalea bushes with only a few magenta blossoms clinging to dense dark green foliage surrounded the trailer. Wilted petals blanketed the ground beneath the shrubbery. The lawn laid bare except for a few splotchy tufts of weeds over the sandy lot. Conch shells sat atop the railing of the small wooden deck outside the front door. The steps leading to that deck were nothing more than stacked cinder blocks.

He moved from tree to tree until he was within ten feet of the trailer, then he darted toward the bushes and wedged himself between a large azalea and the mobile home. The metal building amplified the thunderous drums. On his tiptoes, he peered through the front window.

The living room was empty, with the exception of several large black cases, some round, others boxy, and a large drumset beside a bookcase with a stereo on it and a ton of CDs loading the shelves until they bowed from the weight. Behind the drums sat a gorgeous woman with ivory skin wrapped in a blue and green beach towel, her wet hair was dark, but he could tell it was red. She must be Earl's sister.

The way the young woman flailed her arms was breathtaking. She struck cymbals and drums in a flurry of movement. Her feet worked the bass drum pedal and high hat pedal in concert. The look on her face--slack jaw, head back, eyes closed like she was high on the music--made him dizzy with the thought of how she might look on top of him, riding. He'd have given anything to be one of those drums. She could beat him like that any day.

She pounded the smaller drums in graduated sizes

creating a jungle beat that got faster and faster. Her towel slipped off, and she didn't stop. *Holy, Holy.* Gulp. He gawked at her pale nude body, her perfect sized breasts with just the right amount of jiggle. His knees gave way, and he squatted behind the hedge.

Snap out of it. Stop being a freaking peeping Tom. He wanted to look back in that window so badly his head was spinning, but he knew it was the wrong thing to do. Disrespectful. Invasive. Sleazy.

Jesus. There's a naked woman playing the drums in that room. I'm just a man. A man's gonna look. No harm in looking.

"Don't do it." His inner voice scolded him.

It took all the will power he had, but he pulled himself away from the window and sneaked around to the garage. As long as he heard the drums, he knew the homeowner was occupied. Maybe there were some clues to Earl's whereabouts hidden in the garage. No way was Squirrel actually on the premises. He had to know Trent had figured out where he was headed on the island. Earl wasn't stupid. Well, not *real* stupid.

Visions of the nude redhead filled Trent's mind. He'd walked away from the window, but the sight in the living room was following him around, and he had all ideas it'd become his favorite mental rerun for weeks to come. He'd seen his fair share of beautiful women without a stitch of clothing on, but none of them ever slayed a set of drums like that. He needed a cold shower. Make that ice bath.

With his hand against the hood of an old jeep, he closed his eyes, trying to force his mind back on the game. The hedonistic drumming wasn't helping his cause. He took a few steps forward and stumbled over a tire iron. Arms swatting at the air, trying to catch his balance, his elbow bumped a set of metal shelves. A red plastic gas can slid off a shelf and hit him in the shoulder. As he attempted to catch the can, gasoline splashed his chest.

Ouch. It stung. He ripped his shirt off and wiped at the gas on his skin. When he caught sight of the workroom sink in the corner, he dashed toward it, cranked on the water and cupped his hands under the gushing stream. He rinsed his chest, flinging handfuls of cold water onto his torso. Cold shower no longer required.

A weird squawk came from behind him. He turned around but didn't see anything. Something rammed him in the ankle. Rooting around his feet was a miniature pot bellied pig, white with black splotches all over it, hair so thin its pink skin showed through. It opened its mouth and made that God awful noise again.

"Shhh." He nudged it with his foot, trying to get it to move away, but not wanting to hurt the thing. It let out a deafening squeal.

"Hush up!" Trent ground out. All that noise was going to give him away. He reached down to pet the pig, and it tried to bite him. Trent jerked his hand back. The little ham danced in a tiny circle like it was proud of itself, its short tail whipping back and forth in a blur.

The drumming continued. Thank God. He had to quiet this animal before Earl's sister found out he was rummaging through her garage.

Trent squatted and spoke in a hushed voice. "I need you to be quiet, little fella. I'm just going to put my hand over your snout and carry you outside. Don't get excited."

The pig let him pet its snout then backed up and knocked over a large can of oil. It slid in the oil and made that horrid squealing noise again. Trent found himself slipping right along with the pig and fell. The creature rammed him in the face, its snotty nose smeared gunk all over Trent's cheek. Every time he got his hands around the thing's pudgy mid-section the greasy varmint wiggled away from him. The pig couldn't get enough traction to run, and Trent couldn't seem to be able to stand.

Finally, Trent grabbed onto the bumper of the jeep with one hand and wrestled the pig into the crook of his free arm. The damn thing released a squeal that left Trent's ears ringing. He pulled himself closer to the jeep and leaned against it as he placed his hand over the slimy snout, clamping the piggy's mouth shut, but making sure it could still breathe. "You be quiet."

The drums stopped. Oh no. No, no, no. He took a step forward, slipped, and then down he went, flat on his back. Upon impact the pig was flung out of his hands and landed in a wheelbarrow of potting soil.

The pig got quiet as it rooted around in the soil, all happy like. "Good. That's a good piggy. Stay right there."

Trent rose to his feet in a wobbly sort of way. He grabbed the handles on the wheelbarrow and attempted to push it out of the garage, hoping the pig would remain quiet and wouldn't jump out.

Damn it. He lost his balance, leaned on the wheelbarrow handles too hard, and the pig went into the air again along with a heap of potting soil. Trent slipped and ended up on his back again. The noisy critter landed on Trent's stomach and they both got doused with soil.

"What the hell's going on in here?" An angry female voice boomed.

His face was covered in dirt that stuck to his greasy skin. He couldn't see a doggone thing, but he had all ideas that voice belonged to Earl's sister Mazy.

The pig snuggled up on Trent's belly and grunted softly, seemingly content.

Wiping the dirt out of his eyes, Trent's gaze traveled up the pale slender legs of the beautiful redhead towering over him.

He swallowed hard, and tried like hell not to look up her towel.

CHAPTER THREE
Rooster

Mazy yanked her mini pot-belly away from the intruder. Who was this guy? What was he doing in her garage half-dressed, wrestling this poor defenseless animal?

With the calmest voice she could muster, she petted her pig and said, "It's okay, Rooster."

The stranger's sculptured torso was covered in dirt, but she could tell he was tanned and toned, with rippling abs and those little love muscles near his hip bones that made women fantasize about what sort of exercise men had to do to get *those*. His shorts sagged low and the waistband gaped, making her want to take a peek inside those britches.

Who was she kidding? She wished those cargo shorts would slide right off. This dude was unreal, as if he'd been molded from smoky topaz, or glistening caramel with nuts. Big nuts. Lots of nuts. That dirt was like little black nuts all over his face too. But most of his facial features were unidentifiable due to the mud pie mask he was sporting.

She was nuts to be lusting after this uninvited guest. But one thing was certain, *that* body didn't belong to any local on the island. She knew *all* the locals, and she would've remembered a body like that, and the dragon tat wrapping around his bicep.

He stared up at her. Not saying a word. She jabbed him with her foot.

Whoa. Her other foot slid, and she lost her balance. He grabbed her legs to steady her, but she was already off kilter, arching way back. Oh God. She was going to fall.

The sexy man sat up, shoved his hands under her towel and gripped her hips. His fingers dug into her bare flesh.

What? Bare? Instinctively, her hands went to his forearms to help her regain her balance. As she found her center once more, the towel loosened.

She let go of him to frantically claw at the slipping cloth, holding onto it for dear life, and to her horror, trusting this stranger to not let her fall.

Their eyes locked briefly, but her brain was so scrambled she couldn't speak. He had his hands on her naked flesh. He could probably see all her "secrets" that were inches from his muddy face. She didn't know what was visible from his angle. But judging from the expression displayed in his eyes, her worse fears were probably spot on.

He dropped his chin. His forehead pressed against her thigh. A gust of warm breath blew down her leg.

There was a scab on the back of his head and dried blood stuck to the short strands of his wavy light brown hair.

Lord help her. He's that guy. That guy who got pecked in the head by Spike. Had to be. Same hair, same body. For the love of... She was being groped by the asshole chasing Earl. "Oh. My. God. You're that bounty hunter! Aren't you? Get your damn hands off me!"

She tore herself away from him, prying his hands from her hips, forcing herself backward. Her feet slipped right out from under her. Down, down, down she went, straight to the concrete bottom with a loud, bare-assed smack. The towel unfurled. She yanked it back up, cinching it around her body as fast and as tight as she could. Her back and head slammed against the jeep. Her teeth jarred. Ouch. She ran her tongue over her teeth. No chips. She felt the back of her head. No blood. She'd live. At least she was in a stable position, covered. But Jesus, did she just break her butt? Felt like it.

The bounty hunter's mouth hung open. He was actually panting, and his tongue looked like it was ready to loll right out of his mouth.

She gazed into his piercing gray eyes that blinked amidst the dark mess on his face, specks of dirt clinging to his lashes. In spite of the camouflage of soil, she could plainly see his big ole mouth, big gray eyes, big tree-trunk arms, big...big...her gaze traveled south...yep, big, really big.

Wake up, girl. He's also a BIG sack of shit! And you're an even bigger sack for having naughty thoughts for the man trying to slap Earl back in jail.

Trent knew the young woman must be hurting, she hit the cement pretty hard, and she didn't have a lot of padding. "Are you okay?"

She squinted, her lips pinched into a white line. "No. You're here."

"I mean, are you hurt?"

She shifted slightly and winced, sucking in a sharp breath. Yep. She was hurt.

"I'll make it." Her face became red and tears welled in her eyes.

No. She needed to see a doctor. He could tell by her pained expression. He pushed to his feet and held onto the jeep. "Here, let me help you up." He offered his hand. She swatted it away and turned her head. Women. Jesus. "Stop being stubborn. Let me help you up."

"You're the last person on earth I want to touch. Leave me alone."

He grabbed a nearby hammer and held it out to her. "Now you don't need to touch me. Here." He smiled.

She looked at the hammer and smirked as if she were about to break into a smile, but she turned her head so fast he couldn't catch it. "Smartass." Ha. The tone in her voice was laced with amusement.

The pig snuggled up to her and she petted it. "Rooster, what have we gotten ourselves into now?"

"You call your pig Rooster?"

He lowered the hammer to his side. She didn't seem in a

hurry to get up.

She faced him. "Yep. You heard him. He tries to crow. He doesn't get it right, but he tries. When he was little he was raised around a bunch of chickens, no other pigs in sight. I guess he was just trying to communicate. Anyway, when my friend was moving away she gave him to me. She used to call him Fred, but I call him Rooster. He likes it." She talked to her pig. "Crow for me. Crow."

The pig let out that horrible noise it'd inflicted upon his ears earlier. It did sound like the chubby thing was attempting to crow. "That's funny. You ought to put that on Youtube. It'd go viral."

She laughed. "I've thought about it." She looked up at him and the hammer.

He held the tool out to her again.

She extended her arm and said, "Just so we're clear, I don't like you." She grabbed the claw end while he held the handle and tried to lift herself up without any luck. She then moved her hand up to his wrist for a stronger hold. Her dainty fingers clasped him, and he almost flinched from the electric awareness of her. From a squatting position, she said, "Turn your head." He did. "No peeking."

"No ma'am. No peeking." Little did she know he'd already seen it all, but he'd love another gander. However, being a gentleman was paramount at the moment. The horndog inside him would have to behave.

"Ma'am? Dang, how old do you think I... Damn that hurts." She groaned as he helped her stand. "I seriously broke my butt. I just know it."

"Are you decent?"

"Yeah. You can look now."

He faced her and pulled her to him. She didn't resist. Instead, she whimpered in his arms. Poor girl. "I got you, Sweetheart. Hang on. I'm gonna put you on the hood of this jeep then make my way to the other side and wipe my feet off so I can get some traction." She nodded. He hoisted her up onto the hood and gently sat her down. Her brows were furrowed, but she didn't say anything, just wiggled herself over, inching across the hood with her back to the windshield.

He spotted an old towel on a worktable and grabbed it, tossing it on the floor so he could wipe off the soles of his shoes. She'd wiggled her way to the passenger side of the jeep and had turned so her legs were dangling off the edge. He stepped beside her and hooked an arm around her waist. "Ready?"

"Okay." With her arm draped over his shoulders, he eased her gently onto the floor and scooted the towel over so she could wipe her feet off too. She wiggled her toes in the terry cloth fabric and looked up at him. "You should see yourself right now. Your face looks like one of those chocolate oatmeal no bake cookies."

"You like those cookies?"

"No. I'm allergic to oatmeal. I break out in hives if I eat it. Don't even like being close to it." She quirked an eyebrow at him, coy, as if curious as to whether or not he'd fall for her tale.

"Nice to know. I'll remember that when I make you breakfast."

Her eyes rounded and her jaw dropped. "You..."

He burst out laughing. God, it'd been too long since he'd actually laughed. A real laugh. "I couldn't resist. I was joking. Relax."

She smiled. "You'll never be making me breakfast. So, get that thought right out of your head."

"What? I make a mean omelet. Awesome sausage gravy biscuits. I can even make killer eggs benedict."

"Shut up. You're making me hungry." The pig grunted.

She looked at Rooster. "He meant turkey sausage, don't worry.

They both laughed.

He helped her take a few steps forward, but she was tense. Her pain was obvious. Without asking permission, he lifted her into his arms.

"Hey. Put me..." Her words trailed off and she relaxed, wrapped her arm around his neck and grew silent, her face close to his. The chemistry between them was intense, but she averted his gaze. However, her shallow breathing gave her away. The feeling was mutual.

Without a word between them, he carried her inside her trailer. There was no couch in the living room. He glanced around. She pointed toward the kitchen. "Down the hall."

He carried her in the direction she'd pointed. At the end of the narrow hall was a fairly large bedroom that had been converted into a den. Couch, TV, chairs, entertainment center made from milk crates. Thrifty. He lowered her to the lumpy slipcovered sofa.

She settled in and said. "Thanks."

"You're welcome. Want me to get you something to wear?"

"Yeah." She motioned toward a card table. "Pass me that blue box with the silver bow."

He handed it to her. "Here you go."

She smiled. "Thanks. But just so we're clear, I still don't like you."

He nodded. "And just so we're clear, I like you just fine."

Her eyes twinkled and her lips curled. "Of course you do, Mud Pie. I'm freaking adorable." She grinned.

"Yep. Modest too, I see."

That got a laugh out of her. "Out. I need to get dressed."

Mazy eyed him as he stepped out into the hall and pulled the door closed behind him."

Dang, it'd been nice in that man's arms. Left her speechless. Nobody had ever left her speechless. Being so close to him, he'd felt...right. But he was wrong. So very wrong. Isn't that always the way? The things that taste the best are the worst for you. That never stopped her from eating whatever she wanted, but when it came to guys, she needed to use more self control, especially guys who were after the most important person in her life. Being loyal to family was of the upmost importance, and she needed to keep reminding herself of that. Cause she was craving mud pie right about now.

She ought to kick him out of the house, but knew she might need someone to take her to the doctor. She had a feeling she'd seriously hurt her ass.

If a friend came over right now, she'd end up telling them everything that happened and they'd most likely chide her for letting this guy step foot in her house. They'd be right too. She shouldn't even be talking to him.

She slid the dress she never thought she'd ever wear overhead. The floral, strapless sundress had been a gift from Louise on Mazy's twenty-fourth birthday a few months ago. Mazy had changed her mind about donating it to the Goodwill, because that was Louise's favorite place to shop, and she didn't want her to find it on the rack and get her feelings hurt. Instead, Mazy thanked the sweet old woman then came home and plopped the box on the card table, and there it had stayed.

When Mazy stood, she caught a glimpse of herself in the mirror. Her hair had air-dried and fell past her shoulders in loose curls. Her skin was a pale rosy pink, and the strapless, floral dress fit her perfectly. It was pretty. She felt pretty. She liked the feeling. She'd never thought of herself this way before. Pretty. Her? Who knew?

While Mazy dressed, Trent went to the bathroom to wash up. The hand soap by the sink was labeled ravishing rose. He sniffed the bottle. No way was he going to use that. He looked around the small, yet spotless, bathroom, all done in white with the exception of the seashell wallpaper with a blue background. In the shower, Mazy had five different bottles of fragrant body wash on the sill of the frosted window high above the tub. He smelled each—butterfly kisses, cherry blossom geisha, gorgeous gardenia, and cotton candy. Lastly, he took a whiff of the fifth bottle, eucalyptus. Finally, he'd found one with a gender-neutral scent. He helped himself to a clean white washcloth and towel, then cleaned himself up at the sink.

Refreshed, he strode past a walk-in closet size bedroom, barely big enough for the single bed wedged in the corner. Spiderman linens? Did she have a kid?

The kitchen was ugly. Clean, but puke green linoleum, cracked and peeling from the floor in places? Harvest gold appliances? Wow. Quite a blast from the past, and not in a good way.

He stepped on a weak spot in the floor hidden by a throw rug where the linoleum and the brown living room carpet met. She could use some repairs around here. The eerily empty living room creeped him out. A bookcase and a drumset wasn't what you call homey. She must be barely making ends meet if she couldn't even afford furniture. The oddball stuff in the den looked like she'd gone dumpster diving for it.

There was a room off the living area. Had to be her bedroom. He probably shouldn't look, but he was curious. The door was opened.

He took a peek. Holy shit. She had an ancient waterbed. Those things were heavy. He was surprised the whole trailer didn't lean because of it. Purple bedspread and comforter, must be her favorite color. Old band posters on the walls, probably from her teen years. The dresser top was loaded with perfume bottles. She liked her smelly stuff.

He checked out her CD's. This chic had eclectic tastes, everything from Metallica to Mozart. The CD's were alphabetized too. He smiled.

Gene Krupa, one of the greatest drummers of all time. God, it'd been a long time since he'd even thought of that name, much less listened to him play. Trent's grandfather loved Gene Krupa's jungle beat on "Sing, Sing, Sing."

A goofy ringtone sounded. He spotted a purple sparkly phone sitting on a shelf by the stereo. What if Earl was calling Mazy? He picked up the phone. The name Kendal flashed on the screen. He stared down at the contact list, text messages, and call history. Damn, he should just look and see if he could get some information about Squirrel.

His thumb hovered, but he couldn't bring himself to search the files. It'd upset Mazy, and if the shoe was on the other foot, and she did that to him, it'd piss him off too.

He walked back to the den and knocked on the door. "You have a phone call."

She opened the door. My God she was lovely. A young Nicole Kidman, delicate and edgy all mixed into one. He lost his train of thought.

She gasped and stared at the device in his hand, then snatched her cell away. "Who said you could touch my stuff? Get what you needed, asshole? Write down every number on here? Guess what? I don't even know Earl's number. How do you like that?"

Flabbergasted by her angry response, he stood there with a mouth full of "umm."

She glared at him, a bewildered gleam in her eye. Then without warning, she slammed the den door in his face.

Dazed and feeling like a jerk, he took that as his cue to leave. He walked out of the trailer and down the cinder block steps.

He needed to pull himself off the Washington case. Between losing his mode of transportation and losing his focus by not seizing the opportunity to check Mazy's phone, it was obvious he wasn't the man for the job. As bad as he hated to admit it, Stan might have better luck.

He dug his android out of his pocket and called Jimmy, the bail bondsman he worked for. No answer. He was forwarded to voicemail. Perfect.

"Hey, Jimmy. Listen, I know I already told ya about the mishap with my vehicle today, but as it turns out, I don't see any real chance of getting away from here fast enough to even entertain the idea of catching Earl. No sense delaying the inevitable. Consider me off the case. If I happen upon any useful information, I'll let you know, but I'm throwing in the towel on this one, buddy. All right, man. Talk at ya later."

He shrugged, feeling lighter. Time to just cool out by the beach and figure the rest out later. Maybe that something would include a feisty redhead with a mean drumroll.

Having the door slammed in his face wasn't his idea of flirtation, but Mazy Washington had definitely been checking him out, and the chemistry was scorching between them when he'd carried her inside.

He stuffed his phone in his pocket and smiled.

As he traipsed across the lawn, something scuttled behind him. He turned and found Rooster looking up at him, nose twitching. "Go on back home, Rooster." He knelt and petted the pig. It sat and closed its eyes, enjoying the attention. Trent shook his head with a smile. "Your mama would blister your bottom if she knew you were taking a shine to me." The pig made a faint noise of contentment, half snort/half happy moan. "You sure are sweet. Crow for me."

The pig opened its eyes and crowed. Trent laughed. "I swear, at any moment the Mad Hatter is going to tap me on the shoulder."

CHAPTER FOUR
Band

Mazy finished assembling her drums on stage at Reel to Real Good, a local restaurant where her band played on a regular basis. She duct taped a pillow to her stool and gave it a swat, imaging it was Trent McAllister's face.

Why was she still thinking about that creep? He invaded her thoughts at every turn. All ripped and gentle. Why'd he have to be so gentle with her? Why couldn't he have been a total asshole? And old. And have a beer gut. Anything to make him less attractive.

Kendal, the piano player in their all girl jazz ensemble Bikini Quartet, walked over holding a brown paper bag. "I picked up some floaties at the pier gift shop. If that pillow doesn't cut it, we can try one of these." She dug three kiddie blow up toys out of the bag: a crab, a turtle, and a shark.

Mazy slid a cymbal onto its stand. "Maybe I should stuff my underpants with bathroom tissue like the little girl in the toilet paper commercial instead."

Kendal laughed, her hazel eyes wrinkling around the edges, her face beaming with girl-next-door appeal.

Mazy tested the tension on the high hat pedal, "I've been meaning to tell you, I like your hair like that, the darker color suits you, not that there was anything wrong with the highlights."

Kendal touched her long dark tresses. "Thanks. Mom fusses about it, says I need to have it lightened again. But I like it this way. It feels softer, more natural, less like straw."

"It's your hair, Kendal. You're old enough to ignore your mom and do what you want." Mazy and Kendal were both twenty four, and yet Kendal was still so busy trying to please her parents she hadn't learned how to please herself. That was one good thing about Mazy's parents, even before her mother had passed away, Mazy had been encouraged to think for herself, stand on her own two feet. Kendal, on the other hand, dressed like a granny and still lived at home. But she was the sweetest person on the planet and the best overall musician in the band. The girl could play classical music, jazz music, and honky tonk piano. There wasn't a style she couldn't nail without breaking a sweat. She wouldn't be the first musical genius who came across a little nerdy.

Heck, people probably thought Mazy was nerdy too, with her tomboy ways and mechanic shop, not to mention her pimped out purple hearse. And she was *far* from a musical genius. She couldn't read a lick of sheet music. She played her drums based on groove alone, self taught on her brother's old drums from high school. When he'd gone to jail, she'd started playing to feel close to him. It was lonely in that trailer, her dad on the road, her brother in jail, her mom six feet under. Those drums filled the void and kept her afloat during a time she could have easily drowned in her own tears.

Mazy sat atop the pillow-covered stool. Not soft enough. Kendal had stopped by the drugstore on their way home from the doctor's office earlier, but the store had been out of those special doughnut cushions. It was nice of Kendal to buy the floaties.

Mazy motioned to Kendal. "Let me try the turtle."

Kendal ripped open the cellophane wrapper and started blowing the turtle up, her face red, cheeks puffy. When she was done, the turtle was bigger than the top of Mazy's stool. Mazy placed it on the pillow, sat down, and almost fell off. "I think this one might be too big."

"Why are you sitting on a turtle?" Mazy spun around to see Sam Knight, the bassist, climbing up the stage steps. Her gorgeous British husband, Brock, sat her bass beside the piano, his large bicep bulged as he lifted the huge case with one hand. Whew. Sam was a lucky woman.

Of course Sam was a living Malibu Barbie. It's no wonder

Brock fell for her. Come to think of it, he resembled Ken. Great, now Mazy pictured them living in a plastic dream house together. But Sam and Brock were good people, not plastic at all. They couldn't help it if they were genetically blessed.

Mazy didn't have that problem, however. Nope. Barbies never had wild red hair, freckles, and less than stellar breasts.

Saxophone runs rang from the kitchen. Leah was warming up. Wouldn't be long before the dinner crowd started coming in.

Kendal faced Sam. "Mazy fell today and bruised her tail bone. I had to take her to the doctor. She could barely walk before the ibuprofen kicked in." She tore open the package that held the shark.

Sam smiled. "That must have been a pain in the ass."

Mazy gave Sam the evil eye.

"Sounds like a bum deal." Brock announced with a chuckle.

"Oh, so you're going to get in on it too, huh? And all this time I thought you were the nice guy. The ultimate gentleman." Mazy playfully glared at Brock.

"I'm glad to hear you put all that nonsense behind you," he responded, his green eyes sparkling.

Kendal laughed. "All behind you."

"Your fanny will survive." Sam twisted her mouth around the words. She was obviously well aware what part of the female anatomy fanny represented in Great Britain. Brock looked up at her with big eyes, as if he was shocked she'd say such a thing. "It means bum over here," she assured him.

He relaxed and laughed. "Good to know. On that note, I think I'll leave you ladies to it."

Sam leaned over and gave Brock a kiss before he left. They were so good together.

Mazy was a little jealous. She'd never had a serious

relationship before. Kind of pathetic at her age to not have had a single long term boyfriend. The longest she'd ever been with a guy was just under three months. When he'd asked her to move in with him, she'd panicked and broke it off. Something about moving in spelled suffocation to her. Maybe she was defective, incapable of a lasting relationship.

Kendal passed her the inflated shark. It had a big mouth with lots of gnarly balloon teeth. She removed the turtle and sat the shark on the stool. "Not sure I like where that fin's gonna poke me."

"Tape it down," Kendal said, not seeming to catch on to what Mazy meant. Sam, on the other hand, chuckled and mumbled something about vibrating. Mazy didn't bother to ask her to repeat herself. She had a pretty good idea what Sam was thinking.

Mazy thumped the fin, it slumped to the side for a brief second then stood right back up. "Guess it's been taking those supplements Earl buys at the health food store."

Sam snorted.

Kendal looked confused.

"Inside joke," Mazy said, glancing over to Sam for a shared look of amusement, remembering how they'd once teased Brock about needing a supplement to maintain.

Kendal slapped the fin down and stretched tape over it. "Okay, it's not going to bother you now. Try it."

Mazy straddled the back of the shark, its mouth aligned with her crotch.

Sam started laughing and turned her back to Mazy.

"What is it?" Mazy demanded.

"What a big mouth you have, my dear." Myrtle called out from the edge of the stage.

Mazy looked up and Myrtle snapped her picture. "Looks like someone huffed and puffed and blew your house."

Louise came up behind Myrtle, "You're getting your

fairytales mixed up again, Myrtle. Besides, I think this scenario is a cross between Little Miss Muffet and Jaws."

Myrtle shook her head. "What's funny about that?"

"Nothing." Louise looked confused. "Does it need to be funny?"

"Well, it'd be nice if it were." Myrtle rolled her eyes.

Brock came up behind the ladies with a beer in his hand, "You mean like a cross between Humpty and Free Willy?"

Myrtle laughed and turned to face Brock. "So glad you're here. Give us a kiss." She lifted her chin so Brock could give her a peck on the cheek.

Mazy said, "Y'all are such corn balls. Leave me and my shark alone."

They all looked at her like she'd said something indecent. Then it hit her. "I didn't mean like that!"

Sam said, "Want me to close the curtain and give you two some privacy? How long do you need?"

Mazy closed her eyes and shook her head in defeat. "Y'all are the dirtiest minded people--"

"Is the shark making you feel better?" Kendal asked with wide-eyed innocence.

The crew around them laughed harder. Kendal didn't seem to be in on the joke.

Mazy gave up. "Yes, this toy hits the spot perfectly."

In walked Trent with Carl and suddenly Mazy couldn't breathe. Every cell in her body perked.

The first thing Trent noticed when he entered Reel to Real Good was the sexy redhead behind the drums. Her hair was as brilliant as a new copper penny against the dark blue curtain behind her. The projected words *Bikini Quartet* wavered above her head like a moonlit reflection on water. With streams of lights and fabric flanking the stage, the performance area was classy.

The dining tables were decked out in white linen, candles, and flowers. This place was more sophisticated than he'd expected. He thought it'd be a typical fried seafood joint, maybe a buffet off to the side. At least, the few patrons already seated were dressed casually. He was relieved, because he was in jeans. Unfortunately, they were a little tighter than he liked, but the others in the closet were way too big. He needed to go shopping, if he was going to continue to hang around here.

A petite older woman waved to Carl and the farmer's face lit up with a huge grin. The old man abandoned Trent and met the lady by the dance floor. She jumped and Carl caught her, spun her around, kissing her cheek. She giggled like a teenager. Trent couldn't help but smile.

Carl escorted the woman back over and said, "Trent McAllister, I'd like you to meet the love of my life, Myrtle Pinkerton."

"Hello, Myrtle." Trent held out a hand to her.

She pushed his hand away and came in for a hug instead. With her little face buried in his chest, he looked down at her poofy grayish blue hair and said, "Now that's what I call a greeting."

A twinge of sadness ran through him. He hadn't received a genuine hug from anyone since before he'd bid his dying mother farewell. He put his arms around the sweet old woman clinging to him and looked over at the drummer. She was staring back at him, but looked away as soon as he caught her eye.

Myrtle tilted her head back, "Always nice to welcome a new hunk to the island."

"Myrtle, I'm standing right here." Carl scolded.

"I said *new* hunk. I didn't say we didn't have any old ones. Don't you get huffy with me." She faced Carl with her hands on her hips.

Carl twisted his mouth into a half-smile. "Come over here and give me some sugar, maybe that'll sweeten up my sour disposition."

"I declare, you'll use any excuse to get some sugar." She scuttled to Carl and wrapped her arms around the old man.

He looked over her head and winked at Trent. "Never pays to argue with a lady."

Myrtle stepped away from Carl and hooked her arm in Trent's. "Let me introduce you around. There are several single ladies in the band. They're all pretty girls. The tall blonde is the only one of them that's taken. Just watch your manners around them, 'cause people around here don't take kindly to men mistreating women. I suspect you know who the redhead is, and if I were you, I'd tread lightly around her. Mazy's like family to me, I been looking after her since she was a kid, her *and* her brother." She paused and gave Trent a stern look. "Wonderful kids, both of them, mark my words."

As they neared the stage, the beautiful brunette with the saxophone pointed toward the drummer and said, "You look like you have a rabid vagina."

The tall blonde said, "You'd better keep your distance, Leah. She might be contagious."

Trent wasn't sure meeting these ladies was such a good idea.

Myrtle led him onto the stage. He couldn't help but look to see what this rabid vagina comment was all about. Part of him was grossed out and shuddered at the thought, the other part was repeating the word vagina in a sing-song tone like it was the happiest word in existence. So much fun to say. Say it soft, and it becomes a lullaby. Say it loud, and it becomes a declaration of power, makes you feel like you can conquer the world. Vagina! Say penis loud and you sound like a twat. How ironic.

He peered over a ride cymbal and saw a plastic shark's opened mouth with bright red interior and lots of teeth between the redhead's thighs. "Scary."

Mazy glared at him for a beat then glanced down at the vicious snarl between her legs. "It's a man-eater. Stay away."

Myrtle, fished her phone out of her bra and took several pictures.

God. What else was she hiding in that bra? Saggy old lady boobs for one thing. Maybe he didn't really care what was in there.

"Myrtle, stop that. I don't want you posting my picture all over your blog or Facebook. Don't go getting any ideas."

Too late for him. He already had plenty of *ideas*.

Myrtle put her phone away. And why did he watch? Did he think she was a Ripley's Believe or Not attraction?

Myrtle adjusted herself. "All right, little Miss Bossy, calm down. I know you aren't wild about Trent being here, but there's no need to be ugly."

Oddly enough, he was fairly certain, the gorgeous redhead couldn't be ugly if she tried.

Myrtle gestured toward the drummer. "As you know, this is Mazy Washington. This gorgeous leggy blonde is Sam, her husband Brock is the big guy at the bar talking to my friend Louise. I'll introduce you to them in a few minutes."

The blonde smiled at Trent. She had a friendly manner. He liked her already.

The drop dead gorgeous saxophonist walked over and extended her hand. Trent shook it and said hello.

She had dark hair and exotic features. "Hi, I'm Leah."

Myrtle said, "Leah, this is Trent McAllister. He's going to be staying with Carl for a few days."

"Nice to meet you, Trent. Carl's the nicest man I know. I'm sure you'll enjoy your stay. Feel free to join us for breakfast, lunch, or supper any day of the week. My brother

Jack is the chef. I'm sure you'll meet him before the night is through."

Myrtle beamed up at Trent. "I suspect you and Jack will hit it right off."

The lovely brunette pianist had on earphones and her eyes were closed as she played her piano, fingers flying over the keys. Myrtle unplugged the earphones and the young lady looked up, a what-happened expression on her round face. The old woman gestured for the girl to take off her headphones. She did.

"Little Miss Serious here is Kendal Duvall. Kendal this is Trent McAllister."

Kendal didn't smile. She said, "Are you the bounty hunter?"

Mazy played a rimshot.

He nodded to Kendal. "Yes. However, I'm out of commission right now. Ostrich farmhand would be a more accurate label at the moment."

"So, you *aren't* looking for Earl anymore?"

All eyes zoomed in on him, awaiting his answer.

"When my SUV blew up today, I took it as a sign. Squirrel's not for me to catch."

"Then why are you hanging around?" Kendal was persistent.

Myrtle shoved a hand on her hip. "Kendal, can't you just say nice to meet ya. What's with the twenty questions?"

"Y'all made it sound like we were supposed to keep our distance from this guy and now everybody's all howdy-do, I don't get it."

Trent liked this girl. She was open and honest. The kind of person who had nothing to hide.

Myrtle covered her mouth and snickered. "Out of the mouth of babes the truth is spoken. I'm sorry, Trent, she's right, we aren't too fond of the fact you're hunting one of our boys, but you're just doing your job, and it wouldn't be fair to hold that against ya."

He gazed into the old lady's eyes. This kind of sincerity was rare. In fact, he wasn't sure he'd ever experienced it. His own family held more pretenses than these people.

Mazy said, "Speak for yourself, Myrtle. Some of us might not be so eager to look past his whole reason for being here."

Mazy's eyes bore a hole through him, and he didn't feel so warm and welcomed anymore.

Myrtle took his hand, "Let's go get something to drink."

They walked over to the bar and she introduced him to a few more people, but he couldn't shake off the anger exuded from Mazy. She would never like him. Understandable. But what he didn't understand was why he cared. Why was he so intrigued by her?

All through supper, while sitting with Carl, Myrtle, and their friend Louise, Trent couldn't seem to focus on the conversation. His mind was on Mazy, he caught himself staring at her, ignoring his food, and he'd been famished. But while gawking at Mazy, his fried shrimp had gotten cold before he'd finished it. He'd never let that happen before. He usually ate too fast, too much time spent in mess halls where he had no choice but to shovel meals down, only allotted a few minutes for chow and every soldier had to make the most of it or do without.

The band took a break. Mazy and Kendal were the only ones on stage. Now was just as good a time as any to try to strike up a conversation. He excused himself from the table and walked onto the stage.

Kendal had her headphones on and her eyes closed, still playing her piano. Mazy was adjusting her drums. He cleared his throat. "Hey, the band sounded awesome."

"Thanks." Mazy didn't bother to look at him and was

doing a good job of making him feel stupid for trying to talk to her.

"I see you changed clothes. If you'd told me you didn't like that dress, I'd have picked out a different one."

She looked down at the ripped jeans and black tank top she had on and said, "I prefer playing drums in pants. Dresses can be tricky."

"I see. Well, you still look great."

"Listen, thanks for the compliments and all, but really, I mean...we don't need to do this."

"This?"

"This...this pretending to be nice to each other."

"Speak for yourself. I'm not pretending. I was concerned about you and wanted to know if you'd gone to the doctor today, and if you were badly hurt."

"I went to the doctor. I'm bruised. My pride more than anything. Now, if you'll excuse me, I need to make a pit stop."

She stood, winced from pain, then brushed past him on her way to the stairs leading off stage.

He couldn't believe she was just going to leave him standing there like that. Shocked, he glanced around and caught Kendal staring at him. She wasn't wearing her headphones anymore, and the expression on her face indicated she'd heard most of the conversation. She jumped up and scurried away without a word.

CHAPTER FIVE
Gossip

Kendal burst through the ladies room door and glared at Mazy. "How'd that guy know you got hurt, and what's all this about that dress? He was talking about that pretty dress you were wearing when I took you to the doctor today, wasn't he?" Kendal's voice was high and squeaky.

"Shhh." Mazy looked beneath the stall doors, didn't see any feet. Good. They were alone.

Kendal whispered. "Mazy, something went on between you and that bounty hunter today. How did you really get hurt? Did he hurt you?"

"No. God, no. He didn't hurt me. I really did fall. I swear. You think I wouldn't press charges if he'd hurt me?"

Kendal crossed her arms and raised her eyebrows. Mazy wasn't used to such attitude from Kendal. She was usually timid.

Mazy leaned against the counter. "Geesh. Don't get your tit in a ringer. He came sniffing around the garage today, probably looking for clues about Earl, who knows. He could have been checking to see if I had a used car for sale for all I know. His did kinda *blow up* today, after all."

"Yeah. I heard about that, and I was elated, because it was a lucky break for Earl. But what's all this got to do with your injury?"

"When I heard Rooster making a terrible fuss today, I went to see what all the commotion was about. Somehow that idiot bounty hunter had managed to spill oil all over the floor and apparently slipped in the mess. Then I slipped in it too, hitting my ass hard on the concrete. The really embarrassing thing is that I'd just taken a shower and wasn't wearing anything but a towel."

"You went out to the garage, in front of a man you don't know, wearing nothing but a towel?"

"Kendal, I didn't put a lot of thought into it. I happened

to be in a towel when I heard the racket, so I checked on it."

"Practically naked?"

"Yeah. Dang. You act like I committed a crime or something." Kendal had a bitchy side. Who knew? If the girl kept it up, Mazy would have to put her in her place, and she wouldn't be gentle about it. Normally, she took Kendal's sensitive, tender heart into consideration and was careful not to treat her harshly, but damned if Kendal hadn't grown some claws tonight.

Kendal's jaw tightened. "No. I just...nevermind." She sighed. "I just wouldn't have the nerve to do such a thing."

"Not surprising, you wear a t-shirt over your bathing suit at the beach, won't even let people see you in a one piece."

"I'm modest. Nothing wrong with that."

"Whatever." Mazy shoved her hair out of her face. "Anyway, my butt hurt so bad from the fall, I couldn't even walk at first. Trent carried me inside and put me on the den couch."

"You let that man carry you half naked? Mazy Washington, you have lost your ever loving mind!"

"I didn't have much choice. It hurt like hell to walk."

"I would have just sat there, until one of my *friends* could come over."

"Well, that's you. You gonna let me finish telling you what happened or not?"

Kendal released an exasperated sigh. "Fine. Go on."

"Okay then. That dress I had on when you came over was the only thing I had to wear in the den. It was still in the box on the game table."

"You haven't put your birthday presents away yet? Your party was months ago."

"I put my presents away, just not that one. It didn't come with a gift receipt, so I'd planned to donate it to the Goodwill. But Louise likes to thrift shop, and I didn't want to run the risk of her seeing it. I had no intentions of wearing that dress. Ever."

"Why not? That's a beautiful dress. You're mean sometimes. Louise put a lot of thought into that gift and probably spent more money on you than she could afford. You know she's on a fixed income."

Ouch. Now Mazy felt like an ungrateful brat. "I appreciated the gift. Once I put it on, I actually liked it."

"That guy liked it on you too, I bet. Probably thought you were getting dolled up for him."

"I doubt that, seeing as I kicked him out right after that."

"You shouldn't have ever let him in your house. Listen to yourself. None of this makes sense to me. You could have just called me, and I would've helped you, and you know that."

"Like I had my phone tucked in the towel?"

"You went out to the garage to check on a commotion and didn't even bother to take your cellphone with you? What if you would've needed to call the police? Frankly, it sounds like you should've called them. I bet you didn't even report this."

"Kendal, chill out. Why are you giving me such a hard time? He was the one snooping where he didn't belong. Not me."

"He was snooping, you didn't report it, *and* you gave him a grand tour?"

"Report it? He was at a public business. People come to my shop all the time. What are you so mad about?"

"He's after Earl."

"You don't think I know that?"

"Earl's my friend."

"He's *my* brother."

"Seems like you forgot about that today."

"How can you say that?"

"Cause. This good looking guy comes around and you roll over, like you don't have a lick of sense."

This was so unlike Kendal. The girl was seriously pissed. Mazy wanted to tell her off for being so nosy to start with, but sad thing was, Kendal had a point. The more Mazy thought about it, the more she regretted even speaking to the guy, much less flirting with him. And she *had* flirted with him. Even if she'd like to pretend she hadn't.

She'd let her brother down in a huge way today. It seemed harmless at the time, but Trent had held her phone. He could have found a way to search it and figure out Earl's phone number, maybe even track that number like they do on T.V.

Ever since Trent left the trailer, she'd been thinking about him, and not in the ways she should. Instead of wanting to use his face for dart practice, she'd relived how much she liked being in his arms, the way he'd looked at her when she put on that dress, how desirable he made her feel.

She was ashamed of herself. And the absurdity of her behavior reflected in Kendal's face hurt, because Kendal was right. Mazy's stomach tightened and a wave of nausea swept over her. If guilt were measured by the pound, she had a ton's worth pressing down on her.

"How are you going to feel if this guy catches Earl, and he's locked away for years? This is serious, Mazy. And nobody around here seems to be taking it seriously. Y'all need to wake the hell up."

The blade of Kendal's words sank into Mazy's chest. And the girl had cussed. That was a first. If Earl was put away again, Mazy would be a wreck, especially since she knew in her heart of hearts he was innocent this time.

A toilet flushed. Two small feet in white high heels hit the tiled floor in the corner stall. Someone had been in here the whole time, and Mazy had a good idea who. Someone so short their feet wouldn't touch the ground from a seated position. Someone nosy, who liked to take pictures and spread gossip.

The corner stall opened. Sure enough, Myrtle Pinkerton had been in there. She had her phone in hand, probably recorded Kendal and Mazy's whole conversation.

"Myrtle!" Mazy panicked. "How long you been in there?"

Myrtle put her hand up to her ear. "Come again. The battery in my hearing aid is running low, honey."

"You don't wear a hearing aid."

She grinned up at Mazy. "Oh yeah." Myrtle turned on the faucet and washed her hands.

"Please don't tell anybody about this, Myrtle. I'd be devastated."

"What kind of dress was it?" The smirking little woman wasn't about to show any mercy.

Mazy slouched in defeat. "Myrtle...come on now."

"It was a floral strapless sundress. Light blue with roses." Kendal rattled off.

"Oh, I remember now. I was with Louise when she bought it. I told her you'd never wear it, but she insisted it'd look beautiful on you. She's going to be thrilled to know she was right."

Mazy's face was on fire. "Please don't talk about it. Please, Myrtle." It was bad enough Mazy had used poor judgment and was sick about it, now everybody in town was going to know. She wasn't the crying kind, but if she'd been alone, she'd have broken down right then and there.

"Tell you what. I'll keep this tidbit to myself if you stop being such a little snot to Trent. He hasn't done anything to you, and from what I can tell, he doesn't seem to be too concerned about catching Earl. If he were, he'd be asking all sorts of questions about the boy. He's been nothing but nice, and from the way he's been staring at you all night, he's far more interested in you than your brother. And honey, men like Trent don't come around every day. Mark my words."

Myrtle faced Kendal. "And as for you, sweetheart. Don't be so quick to think the rest of us aren't taking this seriously. There's something to that old saying: keep your friends close and your enemies closer. We can have a much stronger influence on this fella by embracing him than we can by mistreating him. You get farther with honey than vinegar. And that's a lesson worth learning early on in life. So, stop asking the man so many questions and giving Mazy here a hard time. I'm not saying you have to cozy up to the man, but lighten up a little. Carl will keep him busy so he isn't a problem for Earl. We got that under control. He's not going anywhere for a while, and by that time, Earl will have what he needs to prove his innocence. I can feel it in my gut, and I've lived a long life trusting my gut. It hasn't ever let me down."

"Yes, Ma'am," Kendal said quietly.

With that, Myrtle smoothed her pink dress. "As for you, Mazy, I suggest you take a deep breath and relax. You haven't done a thing wrong. If it weren't for you, that fella wouldn't still be here in the first place. You're the one who intercepted the chase. And because of you, your brother is safe right now. So, don't you go thinking for one minute you've let Earl down." She patted Mazy's arm then sashayed out of the ladies room.

Mazy knew Myrtle couldn't keep quiet with a juicy piece of gossip, no matter how hard she tried. But at least Mazy didn't feel so bad about what she'd done, or hadn't done.

Kendal splashed water on her face. When she caught Mazy's gaze in the mirror, Mazy could tell her friend was trying hard not to cry.

Mazy passed her a paper towel.

Kendal's chin trembled and she said, "I'm sorry. I just--"

Mazy pulled Kendal into her arms for a big hug and whispered, "Shh. I'm scared too."

Trent sipped his coffee, rocking on the front porch of the cottage. A pinkish purple sky loomed over the farm. The humid air was warm, but nowhere near as hot as it'd get around lunch time. This was his favorite time a day, when the world was quiet and refreshed. But today was different. Unusually peaceful. He wasn't chasing anyone, didn't have anyone chasing him or trying to kill him, no courtrooms to face, no accusations to dispute, no medical treatment to endure. No funerals to attend.

He'd been to too many funerals over the past five years, starting with his mother's when she'd lost her battle with cancer.

Four years later, he attended the funerals of his teammates, several who'd left behind loving wives and children so filled with grief it was all he could do to keep from breaking down at their side. Those were a struggle to get through, but he paid his respects to his fallen comrades, dedicated SEALs each and every one.

Those men had been like brothers to him. The connection and trust he'd shared with them ran deep. He knew he wasn't responsible for their deaths, but he couldn't help but feel guilty that he'd survived instead of the ones who had left behind so many loved ones, children who'd have to grow up without their father to guide them along the way, mothers who'd never get over the loss of their courageous sons.

It didn't seem right that he should still be here instead of some of those men. No one would have grieved Trent if he'd died along with his teammates that day. His ex-wife sure as hell wouldn't have.

She'd been eager to divorce him as soon as he came home. She claimed it was because he'd changed, and he had, but he knew damn well she'd found someone else while he was away. Hell, he couldn't blame her, not really. They'd married after only knowing each other a few months. Their honeymoon was cut short when he got accepted into SEAL training. He and his ex-wife never stood a chance. The kind of relationship that lasts takes time to build. Time wasn't something they ever had together, at least not much of it. Not enough, that's for sure.

Nope. No one would miss him if he fell off the face of the earth. His father had walked out of his life twenty years ago. He'd never met his father's kin, not sure he even had any. The only family member he'd met on his mother's side had been his grandfather, greatest man who'd ever lived. But a heart attack had claimed his life when Trent was sixteen.

He had friends, but he'd pushed most of them away, except for the man who'd saved his life, Conrad Mitchell. Conrad was on a mission with the SEALs right now, and Trent had no idea where that was taking place.

So, to keep himself from feeling lonely, and useless, he'd buried himself in his work, kept on the move.

But not this morning. Nope. This morning he'd come to a stop, and surprisingly, it didn't hurt a bit. Instead, it felt damn good.

Sitting in that rocking chair, relaxing into the slow rhythmical back and forth, steam rising from a fresh cup of delicious brew, he caught a glimpse of the man he used to be--a fun-loving guy, jovial with a positive attitude.

Granted, his day had gotten off to a great start when he'd woken up dreaming about that sexy redhead, the kind of dreams that put the good in good morning. *Should* he be thinking about her? Hell no. He should be thinking about her brother. But truth was, if he was being completely honest with himself, he didn't give a crap about anything but seeing her again. He'd gladly do whatever chores the farmer had in store for him, on the off chance he'd run into Mazy at some point. Small island, bound to happen, at least he hoped that was the case.

She might have come off a bit cold last night at the restaurant, but when he'd held her in his arms...whew...the attraction had rendered them both speechless. No way was that one-sided. The look in her eyes had given her away. She felt it too. He'd bet his life on it. Something that strong? It was mutual, no doubt about it.

The farmer drove up on his tractor and waved. "Morning. Ready to get started?"

Trent sat his cup down and stood. "Yes, sir." He walked toward the Carl. "I made a fresh pot of coffee, if you'd like a cup."

"Thank ya, son, but I had three cups with Myrtle this morning. She was in a gabbing mood. She talked, and I drank and nodded, which is good, 'cause anytime she's quiet in the morning, I know something bad is on the horizon."

"How long y'all been together?"

"Going on ten years now. I had the hots for her long before I ever got up the nerve to ask her out, though. She had lots of men flirting with her, some of them were rich and powerful. I figured she wouldn't want anything to do with me. When I finally got the courage to invite her to a movie, she asked me what took me so long."

"She's a lot of fun. I can see why you fell for her."

Carl flashed Trent a worried look. "You don't have a thing for older women do ya?" He lowered his voice to a whisper. "I know what a GILF is, and I'm here to tell ya, if you got them kind a thoughts, you and me gonna have some problems."

"Whoa. Slow down. I can see why Myrtle would be just

the girl for you, but I got my eye on someone much, *much* younger on the island. You don't have to worry about me."

"You got your eye on someone here? You just got here? Let me guess. It's one of the girls in the band."

Trent didn't say a word.

Carl beamed. "It's the saxophone player, Leah. I bet that's the one who's caught your eye. She is a pretty little thing, I grant you that. You got your work cut out for you, though. She hasn't dated anybody since she lost her husband. That's been years ago. Sad story, but let's not dwell on sad things this morning. Time to make our rounds."

Trent thought about correcting the man, and admitting he had a thing for Mazy, but decided to let the man think what he wanted. Leah was beautiful. No wonder Carl thought she'd be Trent's pick. If the band members were in a beauty pageant, she'd probably win, but she wouldn't get Trent's vote. Mazy did it for him.

Carl put his hand on his hip and got serious. "I called in a few favors. Got some guys coming over to clear away what's left of your SUV. I figured you'd want to be there, in case there was anything of value salvageable. From what I understand, your insurance people will need to evaluate the damage so we need to keep everything together. It's a no brainer that the vehicle is totaled, but they're gonna want to make it official. Have you called them yet?"

So much for that good morning. "Yep. Called in the claim yesterday, admitted it was my own fault. I'm not expecting insurance to kick in for the damage, but I need the vehicle listed as totaled so I don't have to keep paying insurance on it, or taxes."

"You gonna have to pay it off?"

"Suspect so, but I got the funds. Been working round the clock here lately, Landed some pretty big profile cases, so I'm not sweating bullets."

"Glad to hear it. Still gotta sting, though."

"Yeah. Don't get me wrong. It does sting financially, but it's not the worst thing I've been through. Compared to my divorce, it's nothing."

"Oh lawd, I know that's the truth. I went through a nasty divorce twenty-two years ago. Nearly lost the farm. My ex had the lawyer from hell. I swear to this day she drew a pentagram in the sand and conjured him up."

CHAPTER SIX
Skinny Dip

Mazy poked at the soggy Cheerios in her bowl as Kendal's harsh words from the night before rolled around in her head like a pinball racking up points. The girl had hit an all time high score. Even though Myrtle had helped to ease the guilt a little, Mazy was still sickened by her interaction with Trent. She couldn't eat, which was scary, because she could always eat. It was her favorite thing to do.

The phone rang. She didn't recognize the number. "Hello."

"Hey, sis." Good. Earl had gotten another phone. Trent couldn't possibly have this number. "I got a lead on the assholes trying to frame me. Is the bounty hunter still on the island?"

"Yeah. Where are you?"

"The less you know, the better. I'm okay, and that's all that matters. Has the bounty hunter been asking questions about me or anything?"

A knot formed in her stomach. "Not that I know of. Carl and Myrtle have been keeping him occupied." She hated lying to Earl, but the alternative was worse. He'd blow a gasket if he knew the hunter had stepped foot in the trailer.

"Good. Listen, if he comes around you, be tight lipped. He can't force you to talk. He can't search your property either."

Their mother had willed the property to Mazy and Earl before she died, surprisingly, their father had agreed to it. The land had been in their mother's family for generations. Earl had signed his portion over to Mazy while he was in jail, in case she needed to sell part of it to stay afloat.

"He has no right to be on my land?"

"Nope. Technically, I wasn't living there. If I had been, he might be able to get a warrant, but since records show I was living in South Carolina for the past few months and holding down a job there, he doesn't have any rights to be on your land."

"What about the garage? It's a public business."

"I'm not sure about that one. How would you feel about closing it for a few days?"

"I could do that. Nothing to keep me from doing my work behind a closed door and staying in touch with my customers over the phone."

"Sounds good. Just lock everything and keep a low profile. This whole thing will blow over before you know it."

"Are you scared?"

"Scared about the possibility of going to jail?

"Yeah."

"I've survived jail before. I could survive it again, but this time, what really bothers me, beyond being blamed for something I didn't even do, is the thought of losing the best years of my life. I was just starting to feel good about myself for the first time ever. My boss had recently given me a raise and was talking about helping me go to trade school to get my heating and air license so I could have my own business one day. My boss is a cool old guy. He's planning on retiring soon."

"I didn't know you were into that line of work."

"Well, it's good money. People will go without a lot of things, but they want their cooling in the hot summers and some heat when it's cold. That's high on the list of priorities. In today's job market, it's one of the few jobs you can count on to never dry up. Sure, things might wane when building is slow, but in general, there will always be jobs out there for an HVAC guy."

Mazy smiled. This was the first time she'd ever heard Earl talk about his future, what he wanted to do with his life, his plan to make it happen.

"I'm proud of you, Earl." Her eyes stung, and her nose

prickled.

"Proud of me? I'm in more trouble than I've ever been in. I cleaned up my act, and I'm still a loser. How can you be proud of me?"

"You're dreaming of a future, and envisioning yourself making it happen. You're not in trouble, not really. You did nothing wrong. Everything's going to work out. I just know it. I'm proud of you for pulling yourself up by the bootstraps and making something of yourself."

"I'm nothing, Mazy. But I'd like a chance to change that, and I'm going to prove my innocence. I will."

"Oh, I have no doubt about that."

"Damn it, Mazy." There was a long pause. "I love you." His voice cracked.

Tears streamed down Mazy's face, as her heart overflowed. She nodded, as if he could actually see it, her breath shaky. She couldn't recall a time when Earl had ever flat out told her he loved her. Hearing those words had filled her with such emotion she couldn't speak.

Earl cleared his throat. After a thick silence, he said, "I know, Sweetie. I know. Let me get off this horn before you make me cry too, you mush pot. I'll check in later this evening."

"K." One letter was all she could eek out.

Mazy stared down at her phone, the screen saver of her and Earl flanking their mother, all smiles, her father standing behind them showing off his muscles and tats, being a goofball.

She sat at the kitchen table where she and Earl had bickered often growing up and remembered the time their mom quietly got up and poured a whole pitcher of ice tea over their heads to shut them up.

Mazy laughed through her tears. The house was eerily empty now. Barely any furniture left. They'd sold most everything to pay for their mother's funeral, and Mazy had refurnished the place with discarded items she'd found on the side of the road. Earl robbed the rich and pawned off the goods just so the two of them could pay bills. That didn't seem to matter to the judge though. He socked it to Earl to send a message to others. That and the fact that the judge owned a fancy schmancy house on the island didn't help Earl's cause, even though, the judge's property was never touched.

Earl's drums were one of the few things she'd held onto during those dark days while he was serving time. They were her escape, her salvation.

She had dreams for this land, plans to build a nice brick home overlooking the small creek on the back acre. She'd already started clearing the underbrush and planting perennials. Almost had enough money saved up to move forward with the building.

She closed her eyes and pictured Earl and her father sitting in the breakfast nook of her dream house with a view of the creek, laughing about some of the wild days from their past, being a family again, making her mother smile down from heaven. It could happen. It could.

Earl could have his own heating and air business. She could upgrade her garage. She could make a specialty wing for their dad, so he could have the Harley shop he'd always wanted.

But none of that would happen if Earl went to prison for the rest of his life.

She gazed at her mother's photograph on the fridge. "Earl needs your help, Mama. I could use a little too."

The farmer removed his straw hat and wiped his brow with a red and black bandana. He leveled Trent with an intense gaze. A sadness lurked in the milky depths of the old man's aged blue eyes. "You're really getting the hang of things around here, son."

Noting that the farmer called him "son" quite frequently, Trent couldn't help but wonder if Carl *had* a son, or grandson. "Thanks, Carl. You're a good teacher. Plus, my time in the military taught me how to follow orders to the letter."

"I hear that. There were times during boot camp I wondered if I'd wake up one morning and get a training session on how to wipe my own ass. Two sheets, soldier, folded once, three swipes back to front. Drop paper in toilet. Repeat as needed until no residue is detected."

Trent busted out laughing. "How long did you serve?"

"Not long. Me and Uncle Sam couldn't see eye to eye about a few things, namely my poor vision and even poorer attitude. I'm not proud of my young days, but I sure had some fun."

"So you were a hellion, were ya?"

"Hellion? Ha. I reckon you could say that, but life dialed in a wake up call. Had an accident. Lost my son." Carl's chin trembled. "It shoulda been me."

Boy, could Trent relate to that pain. For over a year, he'd wallowed in the guilt of living when others around him had died. He took a step toward Carl, intending to comfort the man.

Carl put a hand in the air and dabbed his eye with his bandana. "I'll be okay. Give me a second."

Trent was a little disappointed, maybe it was a sting of rejection. Hell, maybe he'd wanted comforting himself and was going in for his own hug from the old man rather than the other way around.

Man up, McAllister.

Giving the tractor a pat, Carl said, "I know what we need.

Let's knock off early. All the animals are fed. Let's go kick back on the beach, have a swim, drink a few beers. What do ya say?"

"I say...Hell Yeah!" Trent smiled.

"All right then. I'll swing by the cottage in about half an hour. Grab us a few beach towels. They're in the linen closet."

Trent didn't have any swim trunks and hadn't seen any in the dresser or closet. "All right if I swim in some old shorts?"

Carl started laughing, looked Trent up and down and laughed harder. "I forgot to mention the area of the beach we're going to is Bare Point, emphasis on *bare*. You won't be needing a stitch, and you're gonna be the Belle of the ball." Carl threw his head back. "I can't wait to see them old biddies faces. Belle of the ball, I tell you. Lawd help me, I'm picturing jingle bells tied to your--"

Trent couldn't help but laugh too, the old man's hysteria was contagious. However, he'd be lying if he said he wasn't stunned, and a bit freaked out, but he was just going to go with the flow. "Jingle bells? Man, you string those around kitten necks. I'd need a cow bell. A great big, deep sounding cow bell. I don't like saying cow though. Do they make bull bells?"

Carl wiped his eyes, still laughing. "Bull? Oh wait, that's accurate. I do believe I got a bullshit detector around here somewhere. I'll look for it, bring it to ya later."

Trent gave the old guy the evil eye then chuckled. "So, everybody goes naked on this beach?"

"Everybody who *chooses* to hang out at Bare Point goes naked. But I should warn you, it ain't the land of Pussy Galore, more like Raisins in the Sun."

Mazy had taken Earl's suggestion and closed the garage temporarily. Her plan to avoid Trent had been successful. The fact that all her gigs had been off the island for the past few days helped.

She stared into her empty refrigerator, her stomach growling. Not quite lunch time, Carl would be finishing up with the morning feed. Not likely she'd run into Trent at the grocery store.

She grabbed her keys and walked out to her hearse, Rooster was hot on her heels. "Rooster, you can't come with me, so stop following me. I'll bring you back some sweet potatoes. I know what you like."

The little pig crowed. She spun around and looked down at Rooster. "Look. I need you to stand guard. Don't let Mud Pie near the house. Understand?"

The curly tailed critter looked up at her with big sad eyes. "Fine."

She opened the back of the hearse and put the pig in a box with a blanket folded on the bottom for Rooster's comfort. He loved going for a ride.

She lifted the chubby little swine and placed him in the box, then grabbed his collar and leash from a suction-cup hook attached to the back side window. After Rooster settled in, she gave him a scratch behind the ears. "If you see Mud Pie, crow. I'm counting on you to warn me. Okay?"

Rooster made a snuffling sound and nodded his head.

"Good, boy. All right then, we're off to Piggly Wiggly."

The small parking lot was fairly empty. No sign of Carl's truck. They should be okay. She walked her pet up to the store and tied his leash to a pole out front. Old man Garret stood beside the donation bin for the Good Shepherd House.

She dug some change out of her pocket and dropped it in the "pot of gold."

"Hey, Mr. G. Mind keeping an eye on Rooster for a few minutes?"

"I always have time for that little rascal." He walked over to the pig and looked down at it. "Well now, you're looking mighty fine today."

Mazy listened to the sweet old man baby talk her potbellied pig. She took out her phone and snapped a couple pictures of the two interacting before she went inside the store.

The first thing Mazy saw when she stepped through the automatic doors was a stack of Island Gazette papers on a wire rack by the buggies. She yanked up a paper and gawked at a large photograph of herself, sitting on that dang blow up shark. The headline beneath the picture read: *Man's Hand Bitten by Shark. Fifteen Stitches Required.*

She'd heard about the tourist who caught a baby shark while deep-sea fishing and didn't have sense enough to cut it loose. Instead, the man had pulled it on board, and the shark bit him before one of the crew-members could net it and toss the shark back into the ocean. The tourist was lucky he didn't lose any fingers and only needed fifteen stitches.

But why the hell was her "shark-crotch" picture advertising that story, like it was her coochie that had gnawed that poor man's hand? This was the work of a prankster. A very short, nosy prankster, or her cherry-topped sidekick. No, neither Myrtle nor Louise worked for the local paper, but they had connections.

Suddenly, Mazy wasn't hungry a bit. She marched right back out of the Piggly Wiggly, thanked Mr. G for being willing to keep an eye Rooster, then walked her pig back to the hearse.

Her tires squealed as she tore out of the parking lot and hightailed it to Bare Point.

Carl pulled up to the cottage wearing a robe and driving a yellow dune buggy. Trent tossed his towels in the small back area of the vehicle and climbed in. "I haven't seen one of these in a long time. This is a classic, isn't it?"

The old man grinned. "She's a one of a kind, I've been souping her up through the years with Mazy's help."

"Mazy Washington?"

"Hell yes, best mechanic around. That girl was offered a job on Dale Earnhardt Jr's pit crew, but she turned it down. I don't know what she was thinking doing that."

Trent grabbed the roll bar as Carl gunned it toward the fuchsia house on the hill.

So, Mazy wasn't just a tinker, she was a legitimate mechanic. She just got a little sexier, if that were possible.

They bounced over the dunes, going faster than Trent had expected, but the ride was exhilarating. When they crested the tallest of the dunes, the beach opened up before him. The sight of dozens of naked, wrinkled bodies was a shock to his system.

Carl chuckled. "Don't worry, give it a few minutes, you'll get used to it. I promise. Just imagine you're looking at a bunch of naked babies, happily playing at the beach, a few in diapers.

"Diapers?"

"Depends, but try not to show much reaction to those. It's a sensitive subject."

They came to a stop beside a large green tent. Carl stepped out of the dune buggy and opened his robe with a yank. His back was to Trent. Thank God for small miracles.

Carl looked back at Trent with a smile. "Lose the shorts, son."

Taking a deep breath, Trent climbed out of the dune buggy, unzipped, and let his shorts fall to his ankles.

Carl laughed. "Look at all them gray heads popping up like prairie dogs. My tent's gonna be popular with the ladies today."

Mazy dropped Rooster off at the trailer and stormed across the street, through the farm, and headed straight to Bare Point.

She kicked off her flip-flops when she hit soft sand. The ocean breeze that normally made her relax instantly was no match for her mood today.

Bare Point wasn't her favorite place to visit, but she'd been there enough times to know what to expect. She could handle it.

Carl and Myrtle's bright green tent had a crowd around it. They must be throwing a party. Seemed they were always celebrating something, anything from a raise in their social security checks to a good sale on that stuff to keep dentures in place.

As she neared the tent, she heard Louise say, "It looks like it's getting pink. Did you put any sunscreen on it?"

Mazy stepped around the tent and saw Louise leaning so far forward in her beach chair she looked like she was ready to face-plant in the sand, and she was pointing at some Adonis's schlong as he stood naked in front of the old woman, drying his hair with a towel.

Mazy stopped dead in her tracks, her mouth agape, as she focused on the familiar dragon tat on the guy's arm. He uncovered his face. It was Trent McAllister.

"Hey, Mazy. We're grilling some wienies. Wanna hot dog?" Myrtle poked Mazy in the ribs. "We need to put some meat on them bones."

Meat, bones, wienies, hot dog. Hot damn, she dropped her newspaper and the wind took it away page by page. She just stood there, gobsmacked.

CHAPTER SEVEN
Kiss

Mazy gawked at Trent. His face turned crimson, and he frantically wrapped his towel around his waist.

Louise said, "I can put some sunscreen on ya, Trent. Come here." She rummaged in her beach bag.

Trent's face contorted like he'd seen a spider the size of a small dog, and his eyes bugged. "No, thank you, Louise. I'm good."

Myrtle howled. "Louise, you'll use any excuse to get your hands on *that*."

Louise grinned and said, "Worth a shot."

Trent backed away from Louise and almost fell over an empty beach chair.

Myrtle grabbed Mazy's hand and pulled her toward the tent. "I'll fix you a plate. I know just the way you like your hot dogs with mustard and chili. You sit right here in the shade." She pushed Mazy down into a chair, which didn't require much strength considering Mazy's knees had seemingly morphed into two cups of jello, and she was too stunned to put up an ounce of resistance.

Myrtle scurried away and promptly returned with a plate of food she sat on Mazy's lap. Carl placed a Corona with a slice of lime sticking out the top of the bottle in the drink holder of her armrest.

In a daze, all she could think about was the fact Trent was...there was no delicate way to say this...hung. Magnificently so. She tried to focus on the food in front of her, because she was famished, but all she could see dancing before her bleary eyes was a naked man--ripped, tanned, water glistening on his skin. And a *massive* cock. Whew.

Staring into her lap, she didn't know where Trent was currently standing. Her eyes weren't doing a very good job of seeing reality, but in her head, he was standing right in front of her, posing for his close-up, inviting her to gaze until her heart's content, and she didn't think she could ever get her fill of looking at him. She licked her lips. Her stomach growled ravenously.

With the hot dog poised by her lips, a shadow swept over her, and she looked up into the sparkling gray eyes of the man from her naughtiest fantasies. He smiled down at her, and it was like discovering him and his attributes for the very first time. His teeth--straight and white, slight stubble on his chin, squared jaw, thick brows, nose a little crooked, like it'd been broken in the past, which she found badass sexy. She stuffed her mouth with chilidog and chomped down. "Mmmm."

He quickly turned his back to her and tunneled his fingers through his hair. When he leaned over to pick up a frisbee, the wind blew his towel just enough to give her a front row seat to the buns of steel show. Another big bite of that wienie. YUM.

She was in a dream, mentally checked out like she'd smoked some of Earl's chronic, the killer, as he called it.

Trent whirled back around with a red frisbee in front of his...footlong...well, maybe not quite that long, but it was like a fish...each time she recalled catching a glimpse of it, it got bigger. The frisbee had no power over her imagination.

He held the red plastic disc like it was a stop sign. Ha. Sure, she should stop staring, stop dreaming, stop pretending she had x-ray vision and could see straight through that frisbee and the beach towel he wore like a skirt. But what was the fun in that?

She reached for her beer. Myrtle snagged Mazy's empty plate and loaded it up again. Mazy didn't say a word, just poked the lime slice into the neck of the beer bottle and turned it up to her lips, chugging down the ice cold liquid.

Releasing an, "Ahhh," she stared at the near empty Corona bottle and chastised herself. She knew better than to drink before food had a chance to get into her system. That typically took thirty minutes or more. It'd been three. The last time she'd drank on an empty stomach should have taught her a lesson. She'd walked through the screen of Leah's patio door, then commenced to wash her hair with the remaining contents of the keg on Leah's back deck. Not to mention Mazy's face had morphed into a "strawberry patch" as her mother used to call it. Face blotchy red like a dingy tie-dye shirt.

However, she didn't care about the consequences of drinking right now. Instead, the only hold on her liquor she cared about was the grip she had on that perfect-sized beer bottle. She ran her tongue around the lip of it, savoring the tang of lime, and indulging her dirty mind.

Myrtle unfolded a chair beside Mazy and said, "Come sit in the shade, Trent. You've had enough sun."

He didn't hesitate to accept the offer, and plopped his two hundred pounds of solid muscle right beside Mazy. She thought she heard him say something, but it didn't register.

She leaned away from him, setting her gaze on the horizon, the pelicans swooping gracefully, catching fish, she kept shoveling in the food, wordlessly. Didn't she come out here to talk to Myrtle about something?

Damn. Out of beer.

Trent reached into the cooler next to him and replaced her empty bottle with a fresh cold one. "Here ya go."

"I didn't ask for this."

He lifted the bottle like he was going to put it back in the cooler. She grabbed it out of his hands. "But I'll take it."

"Uhh. You're welcome." He quirked an eyebrow.

She knew she was acting weird, but what the hell. She didn't know the etiquette rules for interacting with someone her body wanted to jump and her heart wanted to erase from the planet. "It's not like you bought these. I know Carl keeps the cooler stocked."

"Okay, so want me wave Carl over so you thank *him*?"

"No. I want..." Oh she was so not telling him what she wanted, because dammit...she wanted *him*.

"Another lime?" He fished a lime slice out of a ziplock baggie and held it out to her.

She shook her head. "No, I want to eat and drink in peace. That means you and me, no talkie. Got it?"

He sucked on the lime and made a sour face. "Seems a little strange. I mean. Exactly what harm is there in you and me talking?"

She glared at him. "Oh please, you know exactly why I can't talk to you."

"No, actually, I don't. I know why you may think you shouldn't discuss your brother with me, but we don't have to talk about your brother. Unless you want to."

"I don't want to talk to you about anything. Especially, Earl."

He smiled at her.

Shit. Why'd he have to go and do that. "Stop it."

He smiled wider.

"I said stop it!"

He wiped the smile off his face with his hand and stared at her, lips in a flat line.

She busted out laughing. "God. I hate you."

"Well, I don't hate you." He sat up in his chair and pretended to straighten an invisible tie around his neck. "I happen to think you're swell, Miss Mazy." He sounded like Leave it to Beaver.

"Don't. Just. Don't." She playfully smashed her hand into his face like she used to do to Earl, joking around. When her palm pressed into his lips, he kissed it. A tingle shot from her hand, down her arm, and nosed dived straight into her lap. She trembled. Freaking trembled. Geesh.

Slowly, lowering her hand back to her plate, she took a deep breath. She didn't have a brain right now. Nope. Just like the scarecrow, nothing between her ears but straw.

Myrtle gave her another hot dog and said, "Burgers will be ready in a minute. I'll have Carl char one good for ya."

"Sounds great. Thank you, Myrtle." Mazy smiled all zipidee do da, cartoon blue birds singing around her head. Myrtle knew exactly how Mazy liked her burgers, a little burnt around the edges of the patty, just enough to make that charcoal flavor stand out, cheese, lettuce, tomato, and mustard.

The tiny blue-haired woman directed her attention to Trent and said, "How do you like your burgers? I'll bring you two when they're done."

"Thank you, Myrtle. I like mine charred a little too with lettuce, tomato, cheese, and mustard."

"Ahh, just like Mazy. You two have something in common." Myrtle gave a satisfied nod and waddled away.

Dang, he liked his burgers the same way she did. What were the odds? Wait, there was nothing particularly strange about the way she liked her burgers. Still. It was actually kind of cool he liked his the same way. *Should* she be thinking that having something in common with him was *cool?* That would be a NO.

Trent leaned toward her. "You have room for a cheeseburger too? You got a hollow leg, girl?"

She turned toward him and found his face inches from hers. Lowering her eyes to his mouth, she said, "Nope. My legs aren't hollow, my stomach is." Yeah, that was profound. Maybe she should stick to eating and skip the talking. And skip the dreaming about having his mouth on her while she was at it.

"Well, you don't have an ounce of fat on you, so eat up. Enjoy."

"Thanks for granting me permission, your Fried Hineyness, but I don't need it."

He laughed, and spewed his beer.

Dang, she'd tried to evoke her best bitchy tone. Apparently, it was more tease than bitch.

Lord help her. She shouldn't give him the time of day. Should she? Her body was lusting after him. And *his* scrumptious body was practically touching hers. She could feel the heat radiating off his skin.

Oh boy. The beer was going straight to her head. That itchy, tingling thing had begun around her ears and was making its way across her cheeks toward her nose. It wouldn't be long before she resembled a beet.

"You're breaking out in red splotches. You okay?" Trent brushed her hair away from her face. He had a worried look in his eye.

Mmm. He was gentle with her. "I'm fine. I get strawberry patch. That's what mom used to call it. The same thing happened to her when she drank without enough food in her system beforehand. It'll wear off soon. Don't worry."

When she drank too much, she tended to become talkative. She needed to keep that in check right now. The best thing for her to do was to say as little as possible and simply enjoy being in close proximity to the sexiest man in the universe. If the topic of Earl came up, she'd leave. For now, she'd eat, 'cause the food was great. Plus, she had nothing to eat at home. She'd left the grocery store without having picked up so much as a loaf of bread.

The memory of the headline came drifting back to her. Oh yeah. She laughed under her breath at the thought of her coochie being a man-eater. It certainly wanted to eat the man next to her. Rawr.

Trent watched Mazy demolish two cheeseburgers and fell in love on the spot. His ex used to piss him off. He'd take her to a nice steak house and all she'd eat was salad, and she wasn't a vegetarian. She was just always on a damn diet, or pretended to be in front of him, even though he found candy wrappers around the house all the time.

He didn't mind her being weight conscious, but she wore a size zero. He could never figure out why she was so worried about her weight all the time. He didn't care if she gained a few pounds. Hell, he liked women all shapes and sizes. That wouldn't have deterred him a bit. Some of the most luscious women he'd been with had plenty of meat on their bones. He just liked his women healthy and comfortable in their own skin.

Mazy seemed very comfortable in hers.

Watching her eat like a man, this tiny woman, putting away more food than he had today turned him on. She wasn't concerned about being prissy in front of him. She didn't give a crap. She was hungry, and she ate to her fill.

Her tongue darted out to lick mustard off her hand, and his breath stilled. His eyes slid from her plump mouth to her shiny locks. Damn, she was sexy, and she had no idea. That made her even more sexy.

He loved the way she tore into that burger. Was she like this in all aspects of her life? Specifically, in the bedroom. He bet she was a wildcat in bed, taking what she wanted until she was sated. He'd certainly love to find out. Word had it redheads were fiery in the sheets.

And speaking of fiery, she was starting to glow a soft red hue. But he'd take her at her word, that her reaction to the beer was nothing to be concerned about. She should know.

His gaze traveled over her delicate feet with turquoise polish on her toes, over her shapely pale legs dotted with freckles, up farther to the frayed edge of her cutoff shorts and the plate on her lap. She wore a loose-fitting, dark brown Eric Clapton T-shirt with CREAM scrolled across the chest in big white letters. He'd love to cover her chest in whipped cream and lick it off.

She wasn't large breasted, but he could see the traces of her hardened nipples and could tell she wasn't wearing a bra. The contrast of her ginger hair against the brown T-shirt reminded him of the changing leaves in the mountains during the fall, his favorite time of year, and one of the few places he'd ever felt close to heaven. Being near Mazy topped that. She was as close to heaven as he'd ever get, and he considered himself lucky she allowed him to sit beside her, even if she didn't seem to be in a talkative mood.

She took another pull from her beer and the sleeve of her shirt rode up enough to give him a glimpse of a dragon tattoo. He recognized the tat as being identical to one on Earl's arm. "You have some ink. Let me see."

She tugged her sleeve up so he could get a good look at the dragon and said, "This is a replica of my mom's tat. She got it the day she was diagnosed with cancer. Said it would help her be brave."

His heart sank. His dragon tattoo was in honor of his mother too. He got it right after she'd passed away. "What form of cancer did she have?"

"Ovarian. They didn't catch it until stage four, said her chances were slim. She refused treatment, faced it head on."

"She was very brave." He saw the sadness filling Mazy's blue/green eyes and knew her pain all too well. "My mother passed away from breast cancer about five years ago. I got my dragon tat in her memory. She loved dragons, used to collect them. She even glued a small plastic dragon to her dashboard. She was into all that King Author, fantasy novel stuff. She'd go to renaissance fairs and things like that." He smiled, remembering how excited his mother would get about a new costume. "She loved dressing up like a bar wench. I never understood why, but she had a ball with it."

Mazy met his gaze, her eyes darkened to an almost gray color with somberness. "I'm sorry to hear about your mom. My mom died a little over five years ago too."

Mazy's slight smile and the softness in her eyes warmed his heart. He could get lost in those eyes, the way they changed color like the water in the sea.

They had a lot more in common than he would have ever guessed. "Was your mother a redhead too?"

"Oh yeah. She had the prettiest red hair. It was long too. She could sit on it. One time when I was little, she'd just washed her hair and had it flung over the back of the driver's seat. We were at a stoplight in her old station wagon at the time. This military guy pulled up in a jeep beside us and asked if that was all *her* hair. She smiled and tossed her tresses out the window and told him yes. He said that was the most beautiful thing he'd ever seen. She just smiled and drove off real fast when the light turned green. She kept a smile on her face for the rest of the afternoon, even when Dad was griping during dinner. She just sat there grinning, and I knew why. That compliment had made her day. The guy was right, though, her hair was beautiful. I used to beg her to let me brush it and braid it." Mazy looked away like she was suddenly uncomfortable to be talking to him.

"It's good to share memories. I haven't talked about my mom much since she passed. I miss her, and it's nice to...I don't know...just talk about her to somebody who can relate."

Mazy faced him and gave him another weak smile. "I know what you mean."

"So, you were in high school when she passed?"

"Yeah. I was a senior. I nearly flunked out that year too.

Dealing with too much emotional crap to concentrate on school. I'd planned to go to college, but I let my grades drop too low to get into the engineering program I wanted, and we didn't have the money anyway. I was just hoping I could swing a scholarship. Worked out okay, though. I opened up my own mechanic shop, and I do pretty well with that."

"So you're a mechanic. I thought that might be the case when I saw your garage." He knew she was a mechanic, but he wanted to hear her talk about it, share a little more about herself, even though she was beginning to slur her words, and he had to concentrate to make out everything she was saying. It just gave him an excuse to stare at her mouth.

"The Pits? Yeah, that's mine. Self taught, though. I learned everything I know from tinkering around with motors my whole life. I used to take one of my dad's old Harley's apart and put it back together for fun most every weekend there for a while."

A sexy woman who knew her way around a Harley and liked to eat, he was amazed. Overjoyed. He'd love to take her for a ride on *his* Harley.

Trent kept Mazy talking about her mom and some of the good times they'd shared. It made him feel closer to his own mother in a weird way. Something soothing about hearing someone speak lovingly about their mother, someone who had suffered a similar loss.

He lost track of everything around him, listening to Mazy's soft voice, eyeing her pink mouth.

Every once in a while, he shared a story of his own mother, and each time, he could almost feel her presence, as if talking about her brought her back to life, if in nowhere else but in his heart. It felt good. Really good.

Myrtle and Carl started breaking down the tent. The crowd had dispersed. He hadn't even noticed people leaving until now, he'd been too wrapped up in Mazy.

Carl said, "Trent, why don't you walk Mazy on home while I take care of things with Myrtle."

Mazy said, "I don't need nobody walking me home. I can do it myself." She stood up and staggered forward. "Whoa."

He thought she might be tipsy, but judging from her lack of balance, she was definitely beyond tipsy.

Walk Mazy home? It'd be an honor. He hoped she'd let him.

Mazy didn't realize how drunk she was until she stood up. She wasn't to the pass out stage, or to the point where she wouldn't remember any of this in the morning. But she was at the stage that if she'd been asked to walk a straight line, she would've fallen on her butt. Just the thought of leaning back and touching her nose made her dizzy. Wait, she was dizzy even before that thought entered her mind.

Trent picked up her flip-flops and his and held them at his side, then offered her his elbow. She glanced down at his gray cargo shorts. Darn. He'd put pants on. At least he was still bare chested. She hooked her arm in his and regained her balance.

Myrtle whispered in her ear, "You'll be fine honey. You haven't said a word about Earl today. Just keep it up."

Myrtle had most likely been listening in to their conversation all afternoon. Mazy was surprised she hadn't joined in. But everybody had left them alone. Well, a few had teased Trent about his sunburn and made a few playful jabs about it, but other than that, they all just left the two of them to talk in the shade. And it'd been a great talk. He was actually a pretty awesome guy, in spite of everything.

Mazy looked into the Myrtle's kind blue eyes. "No Earl talk. Got it."

Myrtle tweaked her nose. "That's my girl. You'll be fine."

Mazy gazed up at Trent's face. He was looking out at the ocean. There was a sailboat gliding slowly across the water. He said, "This place makes me feel like a new man. I'd forgotten how serene the beach could be. I haven't had much serenity in my life these past few years. You're lucky to live here."

She smiled and thought, "You could live here too." But she didn't say it.

He supported her as she leaned into him and they trudged over the dunes.

A sharp pain shot through her foot. "Ouch." She'd stepped on a wild cactus. He knelt in front of her and carefully pulled the cactus spines out of her heel, then gently rubbed the pain away.

Looking up at her with an affectionate expression, he slipped her flip-flops onto her feet one by one. As he stood and wiggled his toes into his own shoes, he said, "These cactus are all over the place up ahead. We'll have to tread carefully."

"Yeah. There's patches of them everywhere, mostly when you get into the grassy areas."

He paused and bent over to pick a few wildflowers. Placing them in her hand, he pulled an orange bloom out from the bouquet and slipped it behind her ear. "This one matches your hair, like a postcard sunset."

She didn't know what to say to his romantic gesture. Romance wasn't something she'd had much experience with.

They continued on their journey back to her trailer, neither said anything the rest of the walk. It seemed like their bodies were doing all the talking as she clutched the bouquet, her arm linked in his. They were walking into the sunset, across the field. And she couldn't help but imagine walking down the aisle at his side. No, she didn't want to be his wife, but the way they were walking together reminded her of a bride and groom's stroll away from the alter where they had just taken their vows. She remembered catching the bouquet at Sam's wedding not long ago, and wishing someone else had caught it instead. But she was glad she was the one holding Trent's bouquet. No harm in her daydreaming a little bit. Not like they were ever going to be a real couple.

They meandered down her driveway, toward the trailer. Rooster crowed as they neared his pen. "Aww, he missed Mama."

Trent escorted her over to the pig's play area and she unlatched the gate. Rooster wagged his curly tail and ran in circles around them, oinking his little heart out.

Trent helped her up the cinder block steps, to the front door. She felt nervous when she looked up at him, butterflies doing more than fluttering in her belly, more like crashing into one another at top speed.

He held her gaze in his, a myriad of emotions flashed across his ruggedly handsome face. Neither one of them said a word or looked away. She'd never felt so in tune with another person in her life. Never had she shared such intense silence that was able to reveal so much. She didn't know silence had such power. In that moment, no one else existed, just the two of them, locked in a glass-heart gaze. The honest vulnerability both fragile and rare made her sigh.

He lifted his hand to cradle her face as he lowered his head. She knew he was going to kiss her, and she wanted him to, even if she *shouldn't* want it. She did. And the pull was too strong to resist.

Rising on her tip toes to meet him, their lips met. The warm softness of his gentle kiss upon her lips was so beautiful she could've cried. It wasn't a hungry passionate kiss, no tongue, just the lightest brush of skin on skin to confirm their souls had connected.

He pulled back slightly, his lips hovering above hers, as they shared air. Then another kiss, and another. She didn't know who parted their lips first. Perhaps they did it at the same time, deepening the kiss, exploring each other's mouth, until his hardness pressed against her. He didn't grope her or grind. He didn't try to push beyond anything more than kissing. And she'd never been kissed like that before.

It was as if his mouth was saying, "I see you. You're beautiful inside and out. You're a treasure."

That's exactly how he made her feel, like he treasured her company, and it warmed her through and through.

He stepped back and opened the door for her. Rooster scooted over the threshold and sat in the living room, waiting. Trent said, "It's meant a lot to me to be able to hang out with you today, Mazy. I hope it won't be the last time." The expression on his face told her he feared it would be the last time, and she understood why he felt that way. A part of her was afraid he was right. They couldn't date. Not with the whole Earl thing between them. It'd never work. But she couldn't think about that right now. This wasn't about Earl. This was about two people touching hearts in a meaningful way. And her heart had needed this.

She couldn't assure him that they'd hang out again, but she wasn't sorry for the time they'd shared today.

She threw her arms around him and said, "I don't know what happens next, but right now, this is real for me." She kissed him again, and he kissed her back, then pulled her into his arms for a big hug.

She burrowed into the mass of muscle, so protective, loving, and sincere.

He whispered, "It's real for me too." Lifting her up slightly, he stepped forward and lowered her to her feet inside the doorway, planted another kiss on her forehead and said, "Don't be a stranger."

As she watched him walk away, she had the oddest feeling that she'd been a stranger to everyone else all her life, including herself, until today, when he managed to lift the veil and show her who she really was. And she liked the person he'd uncovered. And she liked him, especially him.

CHAPTER EIGHT
Hot Water

Trent woke up thinking about Mazy and their kiss. His body responded with vigor to memories of their heated embrace, which drew attention to the fact he was sunburned. Let's just say...that response brought on a whole new level of pain. And all he could do to relieve himself was to picture all those old people naked at Bare Point, instead of fantasizing about Mazy. This was not his idea of a good morning.

He felt dirty just remembering the nudity he'd witnessed at Bare Point, sights he'd never be able to scrub from his mind. He needed a shower.

When the hot water hit him below the waist, he winced, and cranked the water down to cool. Why didn't he put sunscreen "where the sun don't shine"? Yeah, he tanned easily, but apparently, not there. At the time, the thought of rubbing lotion on his privates, while a bunch of old ladies looked on, felt perverse. Now, the fact that he didn't do it, or at least go into the tent for privacy and do it, made him feel foolish.

As he stepped out of the shower and ever so gently patted himself dry, he caught sight of his reflection in the mirror. He'd heard the term redneck referred to a farmer's tan. He hated to think what choice "names" the locals would toss his way today. He'd endured right many the day before, and hoped he'd never hear any of them again. One lady had broken out singing a modified version of "This girl is on fire!"

What he didn't realize the day before was that areas that were a bit pink in the sun would grow redder hours after sundown. He was practically blistered, well, maybe not that bad, but it felt like it.

The most embarrassing aspect was knowing Mazy had seen him in such a state. But he had to admit, he did enjoy her appreciative gaze as her eyes rounded, her jaw slackened, and she appeared to stop breathing. It was the kind of look his ex wife used to make when she'd ogle a big diamond in the jewelry store. That kind of "I want it" face when directed at him was intoxicating. When directed at his naked body, it was an aphrodisiac.

He hadn't expected Mazy to be so sweet, though. Tough girl, drummer, mechanic, independent, but at the center of her, she was the sweetest, softest girl he'd been around in a long time. A lot of girls fake being sweet, try to act coy, pretend to be oh so innocent, but there was nothing fake about Mazy. In the short while he'd been around her, she'd shown him she had many sides, like a beautiful gem, multi-faceted, and it...well...it fascinated him. He hadn't seen a side of her yet that he didn't like. Every thing about her was sexy as hell.

He rummaged through the dresser drawers. Why did every single pair of pants or shorts he put his hands on have a zipper? Metal teeth anywhere near his crotch right now wasn't going to happen. Maybe he should buy a kilt and fake an accent. Let a little breeze up his skirt as he did his chores about the farm.

He walked into the kitchen, naked, pulled a stalk off the aloe plant Myrtle had given him and cracked a plump succulent limb open to expose the gooey pulp inside. He dabbed his finger in the slimy gel that oozed, then held it to his nose and sniffed. Didn't smell too bad. Not that a putrid odor would have deterred him from applying it liberally to his body. If the most disgusting salve in the world would ease his discomfort, he'd glop it on.

With a feather-light touch, he slathered on the aloe. Ahhh. That was better...

He padded back to the bedroom and stepped into his boxer briefs.

Not willing to deal with a zipper, he opted to hang out in

his underwear while he ate breakfast and drank some coffee.

Two bowls of cereal and three cups of coffee later, he had to pee. The aloe had dried and formed a crust. His underwear was stuck to that crust, and his sensitive skin.

He tugged the fabric slowly. Ouch. He closed his eyes and ripped the underwear away quickly and cried out as if his leg had been blown off. With his palm on the wall above the toilet, he leaned forward and tried to regain his composure.

 This sucked!

He kicked the offending Fruit of the Looms to the side and finished his business. After washing his hands, he went back into the kitchen and located a ziplock bag. He filled it full of ice, lumbered to the living room. He flipped on the TV, flopped his bare butt on the leather sofa, and placed icepack in his lap. The farmer couldn't fire him. He was taking a sick day, damn it.

Sad thing was, staying in meant he wouldn't see Mazy all day. After their time together yesterday and that kiss, he wanted to see her more than anything. But seeing Mazy in his current condition probably wasn't a good idea. In fact, he'd have to be a masochist to go near her. She got him going without even realizing it. All she had to do was smile or eat. God, watching her eat those hot dogs. He couldn't help but wish his dick was named Oscar Meyer.

Crap. He grew hard. He needed to picture a different redhead. Maybe Louise, chubby, wrinkled, had to be seventy at least, and naked as the day she was born. Oh, and wanting to rub lotion on him. There...that did it. Whew. And eww. He made a face like he'd just swallowed some foul tasting medicine, and now that he thought about it, that was a pretty much exactly what he'd done.

He looked through the channel guide. Let's see...Hoarders, Monsters in our Bodies...okay, gross images may be just the thing to help him get through this day.

Click.

Wendy's commercial.

What a cute redheaded actress. She looks like Mazy. Mmm.

Boing.

No, no, no. Not again!

Everywhere Mazy went, Trent was the topic of conversation, and most people seemed to be enjoying having him around, if for no other reason than to have something to laugh about.

Between his grand entrance and the hit he'd made at Bare Point, he'd become Mr. Popular. Popular for being an idiot, and popular for being well endowed. But in spite of all that, most folks seemed to genuinely like him, and it was hard not to laugh at some of the jokes they made about him, or to feel a little sorry for him. He had to be hurting today.

She caught herself smiling while thinking about him and what a great kisser he was, and how the two of them couldn't date, shouldn't date. "DAMN IT!"

"What's wrong?" Leah stepped onto the stage of Reel to Real Good.

"Nothing. I just dropped the butterfly nut to my ride cymbal. Here it is." Mazy pretended to pick something up off the floor and twist it onto her cymbal stand.

"Mazy...you think I can't see that the butterfly nut was already on that cymbal stand?" Leah looked at her like she was an idiot. And...she was.

"Hmm?" Mazy tried to pretend she didn't know what Leah was talking about. When you're being dumb and don't know what to say, play the only card in your hand, the dumb card.

"Girlfriend, something on your mind?" Leah stepped

closer and smiled. "Come on. We don't play for hours. Let's take a walk on the pier."

Mazy blew out a breath and nodded. "Okay."

She and Leah walked toward the end of the pier that was connected to the restaurant. They took a seat on a bench facing the amusement park a few blocks away. The Ferris wheel spun hypnotically in the late afternoon sun.

Leah tucked a hank of dark hair behind her ear and said, "All right, you, talk to me."

Mazy didn't want to be a drama queen, nor did she want to reveal everything to Leah, because Mazy cared what Leah thought of her. Where to start? What to say? What not to say?

Leah pulled her legs up, wrapped her arms around her knees, and tilted her head to catch Mazy's gaze with hers. "I'll start. I've heard about Earl, and about how Kendal fussed you out the other night. I've heard plenty about some of Trent's escapades on the island, including how he played a role in you getting hurt his first day in town. So, I have a pretty good idea what's been going on. I also have a pretty good idea, you're more than a little confused as to how you're expected to feel about him and behave around him. Am I right?"

"Bingo." Mazy offered a weak smile.

"Okay, then. Let's look at the facts. Trent is a handsome guy. You have eyes. You're human. So, for you to take notice that he's good looking is natural. There's nothing wrong with noticing the obvious. Okay?"

Mazy nodded and took a deep breath.

"Good. Now. Another fact. Trent came to the island in hopes of catching Earl, because he jumped bail. Trent doesn't have the power to convict your brother, nor is it required that he believes him to be guilty. All he's supposed to do is make sure fugitives show up in court. You and I both know Earl didn't do the things he's accused of, but let's say he had, would you be looking at Trent like he's the bad guy?"

She waited for Mazy to nod yes, but Mazy didn't move a muscle.

Leah sighed. "I sure wouldn't. I'd be apt to say he was being rather heroic by putting his life on the line to bring the bad guys to justice. Everyone accused of a crime isn't guilty. That's why we have trials. And you have to trust that there's no way Earl would actually be convicted for doing something he didn't do. You could even argue that showing up in court, and letting a lawyer prove his innocence could be a good thing. Running from the law only makes your brother look guilty."

Mazy gasped. Leah was right. All this running Earl was doing might actually hurt him in court.

"Let's look at some more facts. Just because you want to protect your brother, doesn't mean you're obligated to hate Trent. He's a funny, charming, good looking guy, and he's been a big help to Carl from what I understand. Trent didn't have to agree to stay and help Carl out, you know? That alone is testament to the guy's character."

"Stop trying to make him sound like Mr. Perfect." Mazy had heard enough. If Leah said anymore nice things about Trent, Mazy would end up admitting she'd kissed him. And had liked it. A lot.

"Hang on. Let's look at another fact. Your first priority is your brother. I get that. If someone was after Jack, I'd be protective too. It's perfectly understandable that you'd go out of your way to avoid being around Trent."

And that's where Mazy had her epic fail. She had hung out with the man. And she'd kissed him. She was a lousy sister. "I'm glad you see my predicament." Not that Leah had any idea of her *real* predicament.

"Oh, I do. I also see that you're mad at yourself, more than anything else. I've known you a long time. You're always harder on yourself than you should be. You're a wonderful person, smart, funny, talented, a good friend, a devoted daughter, and a loyal, loving sister."

Mazy didn't know what to do or say upon having so many compliments thrown her way. Especially since she'd been just the opposite of a loyal, loving sister the day before. She swallowed down the lump in her throat and stared at the Ferris wheel spinning round and round just like all the emotions in her gut.

"Hey, what are y'all doing out here?" Sam called out as she walked toward them.

Leah waved Sam over. "We're having a little pow-wow. Come join us."

Sam took a seat on the other side of Mazy and draped her arm on the back of the bench. "What's up?"

Leah leaned forward and looked at Sam. "I've been trying to tell Mazy that she doesn't have to hate Trent just because he's after Earl."

Sam laughed. "Hate a man because of circumstances rather than because he's actually an asshole? Who would do such a thing? I never."

Mazy giggled, remembering how Sam tried to hate Brock when she first met him.

Propping her feet up on the rail, Sam tossed her hair back and said, "I know what it's like to be at war with yourself over whether or not to like a guy, and I'm not suggesting you and Trent are meant to become romantic. Honestly, I can't see that happening at all, but hating someone, or strongly disliking someone when they haven't done anything to you, and have actually been nice to you, doesn't make sense. I've been guilty of it. You know that."

Mazy nodded, and wondered why Sam was so convinced

she and Trent were not likely to become romantic. They certainly had been romantic the night before. She decided to not question Sam on the matter, instead she'd just roll with the conversation. "There were times I wanted to tell you stop being such a bitch to Brock. It drove me nuts."

Sam gave Mazy a one-arm hug. "You should have set me straight. I deserved a firm talking to at the time."

Leah scooted closer and hugged Mazy from the other side. Sandwiched between her two friends, Mazy felt better.

"We got you, girl." Sam said.

Leah chimed in. "Yep. We'll help you avoid Trent if you want us to, but don't feel like you can't find humor in anything he says or acknowledge the fact he's fun to look at. We'll help you keep this whole thing in perspective. All right?"

"All right." But what if avoiding Trent was the opposite of what Mazy wanted to do?

Sam asked, "So, have you heard from Earl lately? Is he okay?"

Mazy shifted and faced Sam. "He said he found a lead, and thinks he'll have everything sorted out soon."

Leah nudged Mazy. "See there. Everything's going to be fine."

Mazy gritted her teeth. If Earl ever found out she'd kissed Trent, everything would be far from fine. And if she never had the chance to kiss Trent again, well...let's just say spinsterhood was in her future, cause after experiencing the emotions he'd brought out in her, no other man would ever compare. And she wasn't the kind to settle. She'd rather do without. She'd gone over two years without dating, and it hadn't phased her. She could handle becoming an old maid, but she'd rather grow old with Trent.

The song lyric *I got it bad, and that ain't good* popped into her head and for the first time, she really understood it. The blues. Yep. She could relate. Not feeling free to be with the man of your affection was enough to make a girl feel sad, but having to keep it a secret from your best friends, and worrying that your family would hate you for it...*that* was the blues.

Trent poured the last of the seeds into the ostrich feeding troughs. As he walked by the attack bird Spike's pen, he noticed the gate was ajar and Spike was nowhere to be seen. There were ostrich tracks accompanied by footprints leading toward the cottage. His first instinct was to call Carl for assistance, but Carl had gone into Wilmington to buy more bird food. Remembering how vicious Spike had been the day of the fire, Trent was apprehensive about running into him on his walk back to the cottage.

Every day, while working beside the farmer, Trent had tensed anytime Spike had come near him, even with a fence between them. The thought of being so vulnerable to this vicious creature had him trembling, his ears straining to hear any odd sounds nearby, his head whipping back and forth as his eyes scanned the area.

"Come on, boy." An unfamiliar male voice spoke in a hushed tone. The sound came from a wooded area along the fence that separated the farm from Bare Point. He squinted in the direction of the sound, craned his neck, walked closer to the tree line, but saw no movement, no one, and most importantly, no ostrich.

An uneasiness washed over him. Bad news. His gut never lied.

He picked up a shovel that was leaning against the fence and cautiously walked in the direction of the voice.

Trent caught a glimpse of a tall man's back as the man darted behind a tree. The man had an athletic build and wore a plaid shirt and jeans. His hair was dirty blonde.

Trent called out, "Hey, man, be careful out there. One of the ostriches is loose, and he's a mean one." Judging from the stranger's behavior, Trent suspected this guy was the reason *why* the ostrich was loose in the first place, but if the guy had nothing to do with it, he should be warned that Spike was out. Also, if the guy wasn't the culprit trying to be sneaky, he'd probably respond.

The man remained silent and out of sight.

Just as Trent expected.

Chasing the guy down crossed his mind, but there was one problem, Spike was loose, and Trent couldn't outrun him. Until that bird was locked away again, it was his main concern.

He couldn't shake the notion that this guy had it in for him and wanted Spike to do his dirty work. Trent knew he could be wrong, and hoped he was, but the scariest part about his theory was that it could very well happen. If the ostrich killed him--and he'd googled, these birds were known to have a fierce kick that could disembowel people--it would appear to be an accident. Or at least not a premeditated murder committed by a human. There wouldn't be much of an investigation. That's for sure.

Walking out in the open, rotating to keep an eye on everything around him as he made his way home clutching the shovel, Trent caught sight of the young man zipping from one tree to the next, as if watching, waiting for something gruesome to happen so he could have a nice view of it.

"I know you're out there." Trent called out.

No response. Of course not. Coward.

A rustling of feathers caused his nerves to stand on end. He turned to find Spike stepping from behind one of Carl's broken tractors parked near the back gate.

Trent kept his pace slow, trying not to appear alarmed, but he was. He heard an ostrich had ripped Johnny Cash open a few years before he died, that's why the man got hooked on pain killers.

Visions of Spike ripping into his own chest with those sharp, yellowed, talons made Trent want to bolt for the cottage. But if he ran, the bird would chase him down. Right now, it wasn't being aggressive. It was merely following him home. Slowly.

Trent found a small bag of seeds in his pocket. He'd been hand-feeding them to the hen ostrich named Robirrrda earlier. He carefully fished some out with one hand, shovel in the firm grip of his other hand.

He'd watched this bird eat from Carl's palm many times. Carl had told him if he walked toward the bird, instead of fleeing away from it, it would be the one that got scared and would either run away or lie down and play dead. But what if it didn't feel threatened at all? What would it do then?

Clock him upside the head like it did the other day?

He held out a handful of seeds. The ostrich stopped and cocked its head. Trent inched toward Spike, cautiously, trying to exude friendliness. "Wanna treat, boy?"

The feathered beast nodded. Trent eased over to him and got close enough for Spike to either eat the seeds, or kill him. The bird made a cooing sound and bowed to eat. Whew.

"Aww, hell," said a voice from the sidelines. Footfalls thudded into the distance as whoever had been in the woods fled the scene.

Trent lured Spike back to his pen, continuing to hand feed him as they walked side by side. When he locked the bird away, he reached out and stroked its wings. The ostrich moved closer and gazed at him. Trent saw his reflection in the dark globes of Spike's eyes, and Trent was smiling.

"Friends now?" He ran a hand down the length of the

bird's slender neck, and the ostrich tilted its head back and closed its eyes, inviting a scratch and more attentive petting.

What do you know? He and Spike were no longer enemies.

But he couldn't say the same for the guy in the woods, whoever he was. Trent was a pretty good tracker, though. He'd figure it out, and when he did, Trent had plenty of questions for him.

CHAPTER NINE
Jealousy

Trent studied the footprints by Spike's pen. They appeared to be made by work boots, about a size 11 if he had to make a guess. From what he could tell, the intruder had been around 200 pounds and 6'3" or so. Close to Trent's height and build. He took a few pictures of the footprints with his phone.

Carl pulled up in his truck. "You need to get cleaned up, son. I invited Leah over for supper. Told her I needed some help planning a surprise party for Myrtle. Worked like a charm."

"You want me to help plan Myrtle's party too?" Surely the old man was joking. Trent knew zero about party planning. Well, he knew to have plenty of food and beverage, beyond that, he was clueless.

Carl took off his straw hat and beamed. "Hell no, I just used the party as bait to get Leah over here. Thought you'd be happy to spend some time with her away from a crowd."

Oh no. Carl still thought Trent had a thing for the sax player. Didn't the old man notice he was chatting up Mazy a couple of days ago?

If the sunburn hadn't been hurting him so bad last night, he would've gone to Reel to Real Good to hear Mazy play, and to try to squeeze in a little conversation between sets. Lovely as Leah was, she didn't trip his trigger.

"Well, ain't ya gonna say something?" Carl looked confused.

"I'm not into being set up. I like to handle things my own way."

"Well, you can handle it this evening. Myrtle's gone to Wilmington with Louise on a shopping spree, and I could use a hand cooking supper. I bought us some steaks, potatoes, and salad fixings. Should be pretty easy. You told me you liked to cook, so I thought for sure you wouldn't mind helping out." Carl was practically pouting.

He couldn't leave the guy hanging. And until Mazy gave Trent the green light, he figured he'd be better off keeping their private life...private. However, having dinner with Carl and Leah would mean missing an opportunity to see Mazy for the second night in a row.

Maybe he could cook the steaks and make an excuse to leave without eating. Carl looked worried. Poor guy. Okay. He caved. He didn't have the heart to let the man down.

"No problem, man. I'll be happy to grill the steaks, if you can handle the salad. We'll nuke the potatoes in the microwave."

"Sounds good. She'll be here around six. We still got a couple hours. I thought you might want some new duds, so I took the liberty of picking you up something from the Goodwill. Everything's brand new, still got the tags." Carl passed Trent a plastic bag.

He looked inside and tried to act pleased. A button-down with a sailboat motif, a pair of tan polyester slacks, and a striped elastic belt. Great. His flip-flops would really set off the ensemble, make everything "pop". Not. He closed his eyes and tried to think of just the right thing to say without hurting Carl's feelings.

"Thanks, Carl. You have quite a sense of fashion."

"Oh, I know. Let me tell you something. Shirts with anything nautical on them are the thing around here. Tropical printed floral ones are tacky, though, so steer clear of them, but fish or boats. Man, that's the ticket. I was surprised somebody hadn't snapped that one up already. Must've just put it out today. Those kind go fast. I was a little sad it was too big for me, to tell ya the truth. But it's gonna look great on you. Wait and see."

Trent searched his mind for the perfect response and came up with...nothing. Nope. Not a thing.

As the farmer sat a couple bags of seeds by the gate, Trent said, "Somebody let Spike out of his pen while you were gone."

Carl straightened. He didn't appear alarmed, though. "Were they riding him?"

"No. They just let him out."

"Did you talk to them?"

"Nope. They hid from me. I lured Spike back and locked him up."

"Was probably Rudy, coming to train for the race. He's the best jockey around. Wins most every time."

"Y'all race these birds like horses?"

"Hell yeah. Island Riders is the number one ostrich racing league in the whole U.S. of A."

"I'd love to see that."

"Stick around. We got a big race coming up in another month or two."

Trent felt a twinge of sadness, cause he doubted he'd be hanging around two months from now, unless something developed between him and Mazy. Then, nothing would be able to pull him away.

Trent nodded. "So, does this Rudy fella have a last name?"

"Cannon. Rudy Cannon's his name. Little bitty fella, not much bigger than Myrtle."

Nope. Not the right guy. Damn. "No couldn't have been Rudy then. This guy was about my size with dirty blonde hair."

Carl looked Trent up and down as if he were sizing him up. "Could have been Dirk or his brother Ted. They've been trying to train Spike to do some tricks. They want to enter him in some kind of show. I think they've lost their minds. But, Spike seems to be catching on. Kinda surprised me. He can do the gallop step pretty well now."

Trent tried to picture Spike being paraded around an arena like a show pony, but found himself fearing for the onlookers, cause there was no telling when Spike would morph into a Spikeasaurus Rex. Gave him the jeebies just imagining it. "Is it okay for these guys to come in here and let Spike out like that? What if he attacked somebody?"

"Attack? You mean like he went after you the other day?"

"Yeah."

"That was an unusual circumstance. He was defending his territory. You came flying through here then set the place on fire. And he'd never seen ya. You've been working with these birds for days now. Spike knows you're not a threat. He ain't nothing to worry about. You saw for yourself."

The bird had been remarkably easy to manage. "So, there's no chance somebody let Spike out to mess with me?"

"Mess with *you*? What on earth for? No, I usually let Spike run around the farm all he wants. Whoever it was probably didn't think much about it. Certainly not trying to get you hurt. You're being paranoid." Carl shoved his hand on his hip and held Trent's gaze. "Listen here, the only reason I kept Spike locked up is so you'd feel more comfortable. You act right skittish around him. I figured it stemmed from the way the two of you met, but I think it's time I start letting you work with him. It'll help you overcome your fear."

Maybe Carl had a point, but something seemed fishy about the way the guy hid from Trent today. Dirk and Ted. He'd do a little digging on those two, see what he could find out.

Mazy stared into her closet, eyeing the floral sundress Louise had given her. She knew Louise would be thrilled to see her wear it. But Mazy was still disappointed that Trent hadn't shown up at the gig a couple of nights ago, when she'd gotten dressed up in case she ran into him. The idea of getting gussied up again tonight seemed pointless. He hadn't made an effort to see her in two days, going on three. Guess that kiss hadn't meant that much to him.

But the memory of it penetrated her thoughts, even when she was doing the most mundane things. And each time she revisited the moment in her mind, her body responded as if he were right there, kissing her for real. She was obsessed. There was no other way to describe it. His lips were like the moon pulling the tide in her, her heart and desire swelling with anticipation for their next meeting. The fact that she hadn't seen him since, left her yearning to the point she would surely burst. And it scared the shit out of her.

It had been a sweet goodnight kiss. "Don't be a stranger." He'd as good as said, "See ya around, kid."

What was wrong with her? How could one romantic encounter with this man, a man she had no business being with, take root inside her with such force that it was all she wanted to think about? And it had her dreaming of what it would be like to be loved completely by him, and to give herself over to the tidal wave of emotion his tenderness evoked in her.

It was a kiss for heaven's sake. She'd been kissed before.

But this was different. It felt so...so...what? Two souls soldered together at the lips? God. She really needed help with this girlie shit. Even when she tried to think all rainbows and butterflies it came out exhaust pipes and hubcaps.

He had her feeling utterly mushy, and it was uncharted territory for her. She ran her hand down the length of the cotton garment. Had his mouth been some sort of drug, transforming her into some dainty, starry-eyed woman she didn't recognize? She wasn't this...this...feminine, was she?

Why was she so drawn to this freaking tea party frock? Wasn't she too *Rosie the Riveter* for this *Tip Toe Through the Tulips* dress?

What was wrong with her? She'd never agonized over clothes before. She'd always worn whatever she wanted, because it suited her mood.

She balled her fist and released a frustrated groan.

Screw it. She was in the mood to be the rose garden instead of the manure for a change.

Kendal was warming up on stage when Mazy arrived. Her friend looked up from the piano keys, and her mouth fell open. "Look at you! Louise is going to be so happy."

Mazy touched her mother's pearl necklace. She could almost sense her mother smiling down on her with approval. For the first time in her life, Mazy felt elegant, special, almost royal, not that she had any idea what royal felt like.

Who did she think she was? Queen of the Junkyard? Maybe she needed an air filter for a crown and a tire iron for a sceptre?

Kendal glanced down at her own brown sack dress and said, "I think I need to go shopping. You make me look like I raided a monk's closet and didn't even bother grabbing the rope belt."

Sadly that image was spot on. Poor girl. "Anytime you want to go, I'm game." Mazy would love to see Kendal come out of her shell and embrace her curvy figure, stop letting her prudish mother dictate her every move and what she wore. Kendal was too old for that. It was time.

Sam and Leah chatted as they walked toward the stage. Leah's arms were waving in animated conversation, and she had a huge grin on her face.

When the women got close enough to be heard, Leah said, "He needs a little help in the clothes department. I mean, he was dressed like my sixty year old uncle, but somehow he managed to still look cute. Oh, and he can cook a mean steak. Mine was done to perfection. You know how picky I am. Jack has spoiled me."

Sam replied. "Men who can cook are the best. I love the fact Brock is an awesome chef. If we had to survive on my skills in the kitchen, we'd be dead by now. Case in point, I tried to impress him and cook a turkey breast last Sunday. I read the cooking instructions. There was nothing on there about thawing it first. And I couldn't figure out why there was this plastic blue thing was stuck in the meat. Who wants to eat plastic? Took me thirty minutes to dig that thing out with an ice pick. Put the turkey breast in the oven for five hours at 275 degrees. Took it out and the damn thing was still frozen. Brock laughed at me. Then he saw the ice pick and that do-flotchy and informed me I'd removed the pop-up timer that indicates when the bird is done."

Leah laughed. "Oh my God. You have got to tell Jack that story." She brushed her dark hair from her eyes. "Dustin was useless in the kitchen. He tried to make pesto once, because it required no cooking. The recipe called for three cloves of garlic. So he peeled three heads of garlic, thinking a head was a clove, mashed everything up. We both had garlic breath for a week. I kid you not." Her face shined with the joy brought on by the fun memory, and then she suddenly became somber.

Mazy hadn't heard Leah mention her husband's name in quite a while. He'd died in a car crash several years ago. Leah hadn't dated anyone since. Maybe she'd finally found someone she liked well enough to take a chance. It'd be good for her. She deserved to find happiness again.

Sam put her arm around Leah. "Dustin was perfect for you. He'd want you to have fun. I think it's great you had a good time last night."

Leah nodded. "I wouldn't call last night a date. However, Trent *is* a great guy. But someone needs to inform him polyester pants are a form of birth control."

Sam burst out laughing.

Mazy was too stunned to hear Trent's name to find anything funny.

Trent? Had Leah gone out with Trent McAllister? She could think of all kinds of creative forms of "birth control" for that hound dog. She envisioned a pair of steel desktop clacker balls hung from her rearview mirror like fuzzy dice. And it would only take a little dollop of crazy glue to make sure he keeps his shooter in his pants.

She'd let herself obsess about someone who had no qualms about kissing her one night and going out with one of her best friends two nights later?

A cold sweat broke out across her brow, as she ground her teeth to keep from screaming. She was either going to be sick or detonate right there on the stage.

Speak of the devil, in walked the hound dog himself with Carl. Mazy locked her gaze with his, wishing she could shoot poisoned darts through with her eyes.

He smiled.

She did not. In fact, she hoped the expression on her face conveyed the sheer fury raging within her.

Leah waved to him. He waved back to *her.*

Instead of becoming madder, his actions hurt her heart. Her nostrils flared and her eyes stung. Be damned if she'd shed a tear. She steeled herself. This wasn't a game she was interested in playing.

Leah didn't know she had kissed Trent. She didn't have the slightest notion Mazy had even so much as fantasized about him. She couldn't be mad at *her.* But she sure as hell could despise *him.*

A man would *not* come between her and one of her

dearest friends, and certainly no man would come between her and her family.

That settles that. She clamped her eyes shut. Poof. She plucked all thoughts of being with Trent out of her head. Just like that. Gone. He didn't exist. He was now a ghost only visible to those who had the slightest interest in him. And the only interest she had in him was how fun it would be to roast him over an open fire.

Trent was too distracted by the fact Mazy was ignoring him to focus on whatever Carl was trying to tell him. She avoided making eye contact, but he knew she saw him the minute he walked in. He caught her staring right at him, and that stare had been so filled with venom it'd damn near paralyzed from thirty feet away. As soon as he'd smiled, she'd turned away and busied herself, letting her gaze absently travel all over the restaurant, but somehow managing to bypass him. Did she really think he didn't know the "invisible man" game? Women always pulled that shit so the guy will come up and ask what's wrong, only to be told "nothing", or worse "everything's fine."

But he had a remedy for that disease. Don't act like you notice you are being ignored, and don't ask what's wrong. Women hated when you did that, but the trick never failed.

Pissy or not, Mazy looked gorgeous wearing the dress he'd dreamed of peeling off of her the first day they met. He could understand her being a little miffed that he hadn't come by or made a point to see her since their kiss, but this cold treatment--make that liquid nitrogen--was a little hardcore for simply not seeing or talking for a couple of days.

Myrtle wrapped her arms around his waist and said, "MmmMmm, I could get used to this. You're the perfect cuddling size."

He smiled down at her and put his arms around her. "And you're the perfect cuddling partner. I could fit you in my pocket and carry you around with me all day long."

She eyed the front pocket of his jeans and grinned. "That could be fun."

Carl cleared his throat and cast a scowl toward Trent. Myrtle pulled back, rolled her eyes at the farmer, and said, "Oh shoo, don't you even try it, Mister. You know you're the only man I do more than cuddle with." She winked at Trent.

Carl put a finger to his mouth. "Nobody needs to know our business, you little wildcat." He popped her on the butt with an opened palm.

She grinned. "Is that foreplay?"

Trent shook his head, trying to rattle that image out of his mind. "Excuse me, I think I'm gonna go get a drink. I'll meet up with you two later on."

Myrtle studied his face, looked toward the stage, then back at Trent. She smirked. "Red's in a mood. Good luck."

Trent tried to convey a calm demeanor, as if he hadn't noticed the ice Mazy was throwing at him. He gave Jack an upward nod and pulled himself up to the bar. Jack walked over, drying a martini glass. "Hey, man. I heard about your 'over exposure'. Doing all right?"

The indecent sunburn was not the thing Trent wanted to discuss, but seemed to be everyone else's favorite topic. "I'm much better now."

"Glad to hear it. That had to hurt." Jack sucked in a breath with a hiss and shuddered. "By the way, Leah said you're a top-notch cook. Said you could give me a run for my money when it comes to steak."

"Your sister exaggerates. All I did was toss some steaks on the grill with a dash of salt and pepper and some crushed garlic."

"Lightly seasoned and grilled to perfection is hard to beat." He sat the glass down and placed his hands on the counter and leaned forward. "What are ya drinking tonight? On me."

"Thanks, but you don't need to do that. I can pay."

"My pleasure. It was nice to see Leah smiling today."

Oh no. Had Leah gotten the wrong impression last night? Carl made some excuse about having to help a friend whose car broke down and left Trent no choice but to have dinner with her alone. But they hadn't been flirting. At least he hadn't been, and he didn't get that vibe from her either.

"Doesn't she usually smile?" Trent tried to act nonchalant.

"Well, yeah, when it comes to friends and family, but she hasn't had dinner with a guy in years. My wife and I have offered to set her up many times, but she refuses."

"So, she views last night as a--"

Jack raised his brows. "Oh, nah, I didn't mean it like that. She made it clear that you weren't the one who invited her to dinner. She didn't call it a date, but now that she sees spending an evening with a man she doesn't know very well isn't such a bad thing, maybe she'll be more open to dating in the future. I didn't mean to make you uncomfortable."

"No. I'm good. I just wanted to make sure that, uhh, well, you know."

"Gotcha. If I thought you were leading my sister on, I wouldn't be friendly, that's for sure. So, drink?"

"Whiskey Sour."

"Coming right up." Jack cast a glance toward the door and nodded to whoever walked in. Trent turned and saw a young man who resembled the guy in the woods the day before.

Trent pointed toward the man who'd just entered the

restaurant and was heading toward the stage. "I've seen that guy around, but I can't remember his name."

"Ted Davis. He's a decent carpenter. Has an engineering degree from North Carolina State University, but seems content doing odd jobs here on the island. I think he's just hanging around to keep an eye on his folks. His dad was diagnosed with early onset Alzheimers. He and his brother have been helping their mom out as much as they can, so their dad doesn't have to be put in a nursing home. Their good guys, both of them."

"Is his brother here now?"

"Yeah, Dirk's over there by the jukebox."

That guy's hair was buzzed. Nope. Not the fella from the woods. Ted was his man.

But the touching tidbit Jack shared about the guys threw Trent off. He'd planned to confront the intruder about the sneaky incident at the farm, but between the way Carl made it seem like no big deal and Jack revealed some information that made Trent want to actually like Ted and his brother...hmm...Trent wasn't quite sure what to do.

Ted bumped into a table as he walked toward the bar, his attention on the girls in the band.

Trent's gaze drifted to Mazy. She still wouldn't look at him. Fine.

He turned so his back was to Ted, and kept an eye on him via the reflection in the mirror behind the liquor bottles.

There was only one available barstool, and it was next to Trent. Perfect.

CHAPTER TEN
Jellyfish

Mazy watched Ted belly up to the bar right beside Trent. A wicked thought flashed through her mind. Ted had been trying to get her to go out on a date with him for two years. Maybe tonight would be his lucky night. She could give Trent a taste of his own medicine.

She walked up behind the two men and tapped Ted on the shoulder. He spun around with a goofy grin on his face.

"Why, Miss Mazy Washington, you're looking beautiful this evening." He pulled her in for a big bear hug.

She looked over Ted's shoulder, straight into Trent's gray eyes. So that's what a man looks like when he's been smacked in the back of the head with a proverbial frying pan. Awesome. His jaw muscles flexed and a single brow lifted in a disapproving arc, but his controlled movements couldn't hide the fact somewhere deep inside him a switch had been flipped and he was now eyeing Ted through the scope of a mental rifle.

A zing of satisfaction whipped through her as she read his "what do you think you're doing" expression loud and clear. And it was apparent he had no more clue what hit him than she did when Leah came in this evening, talking about the great dinner she and Trent had shared the night before.

Ted pulled back and held her an arm's length away. "I must say, I never would have imagined seeing you in a dress like this, but it looks great. You look amazing. Girl, you got my head spinning so fast, I can't even think straight."

Keep it coming Ted. Lay it on thick as you can.

She tossed her hair coyly. "I am a girl, in spite of popular belief." Move over Scarlet O'Hara.

"I've always known that. As you recall, I've had my eye on you for quite a while. And the offer still stands." Ted stood and ushered her to take his seat.

She slid onto the barstool, keeping her back to Trent,

even though the nearness of him was like holding her hand over an open flame. She wouldn't allow herself to show any outward reaction to his presence. Instead, she flirted with Ted as hard as she could. "What offer is that, Ted?"

"Dinner, movie, anything you want. Your choice. Any time your little heart desires." He placed a hand on the small of her back and cast a smirk Trent's direction.

Oh, good move, Ted. Did he know she and Trent had a "moment" together the other day? She hoped not.

Leah walked up to Trent. "Good to see ya, Trent. I really enjoyed dinner last night. I've been bragging on you all day."

Mazy positioned herself so she could see Leah out of the corner of her eye. Leah rested a hand on Trent's bicep and gave a little squeeze, but she seemed pretty casual. Not particularly flirty. But Mazy had never witnessed Leah flirting before, so maybe playing it cool was her style.

Trent said, "You'll have to thank Carl for that. All I did was work the grill." In the reflection of the bar mirror she noticed he looked over at her as he said that, as if making sure she heard him. She looked straight ahead without acknowledging him.

Ted draped his arm around Mazy. Normally she would have shimmied away from him. She liked Ted, as a friend, but she had zero interest in dating him. Honestly, she couldn't figure out why he'd kept pursuing her for so long when he was such a good looking guy and plenty of women would love to go out with him.

Leah tapped Ted on the shoulder, "Mind if I borrow Mazy from you for a few minutes?"

Ted pouted. "Can it wait?"

Leah gave him a teacher's scowl.

"All right. Fine." He whispered in Mazy's ear, "I'll call you later." Then he backed up so she could follow Leah to the stage.

Mazy gave a glance over her shoulder, expecting to see Trent watching her, but he was gone. An empty glass and some cash sat on the counter where he'd been. She whirled around and eyed the door just as he exited without looking back.

Why didn't she feel like gloating? Instead, she felt downright nauseous. Guilt? Frustration? Both?

Leah pulled her to the corner of the stage. "Answer me one question. Are you genuinely interested in going out with Ted Davis?"

Mazy glared at Leah. What right did she have to demand an answer to that question when she'd gone out with Trent? Okay, so Leah had no idea Mazy and Trent had a thing going on, if you could call their kiss a thing, but still.

Mazy looked over at Ted who was smiling back at her, staring as if she was the only person in the room. Crap. She'd led him on. How was she going to get out of a date with him now? Maybe she'd just go. Make him miserable to be with her and then he'd get over his little crush, if that's what you'd call it.

Leah crossed her arms in front of her chest. "Well?"

"Is that any of your business?" Mazy quipped. She loved Leah, but whoever was possessing Leah's body right now, she felt no love for whatsoever.

"I've got no issues with you dating Ted. None. But I do have a problem with you toying with his emotions. And more than that, I have a huge problem with you messing with Kendal's."

"Kendal? What the hell does she have to do with this?"

Leah relaxed her arms. "I thought that's why you never went out with Ted, because you knew Kendal had a thing for him."

"Kendal hasn't ever said anything of the kind to me. What makes you think that?"

"She told me so. She confided to me that she's been pining away for Ted while you couldn't care less about him."

"Why didn't she tell me this? I could have helped her hook up with him. Maybe."

"Cause Ted has eyes for you. No one wants to be second best. She'd accepted the fact that he liked you and not her. But if you start playing head games with him, when you aren't seriously interested in him, it's going to upset her."

"Heck, the way she blessed me out about Earl I thought maybe she had the hots for *him*."

Leah smiled. "Kendal and Earl? Come on, now. They are like brother and sister. If someone was after you, she would've been just as angry. When other kids teased her, called her Tootsie Roll in school, who took up for her?"

Mazy remembered how cruel the other kids had been to Kendal. She wasn't really fat, just a little chunky, but because she was an easy target, some of the other kids couldn't resist taking a pop shot every chance they had.

"Earl and I always defended her."

"Right. So, you can understand why she was protective of him. Ted is a different matter. She's shy. Ted has never so much as given her a second glance, but he's been chasing you for nearly two years. How do you think that makes her feel?"

"Well, she should have said something. Besides, if she would stop hiding in those sack dresses, Ted might look at her. She's pretty. She just doesn't know it."

"Would you have said something if a guy was all into her and not paying you any mind, and you had a crush on him?"

Mazy thought about it. If she had a crush on a guy who didn't seem to even notice her, she'd probably act like she didn't notice him right back and never tell a soul. If that guy was flirting with one of her closest friends, she'd probably do everything in her power to hide her attraction for him, so that her jealousy didn't end up making a fool of her.

Mazy felt bad. How many times had Kendal been with her when Ted had flirted his butt off? That must have been hard for her to witness, but she never said a word about it. If anything, she'd occasionally say a kind word about Ted and ask Mazy why she didn't take him up on his offer.

Leah patted Mazy's arm. "It's okay. You didn't know. Now you understand my concern. If you want to date Ted, that's fine, but if you're just playing games, that's not fair to him or Kendal, and they are both good people."

It dawned on Mazy that Leah must have some reason she thought Mazy wasn't serious about Ted. "What makes you think I'm playing games?"

She smiled. "Because I see the way you look at Trent. The way he looks at you, and you were all he wanted to talk about last night when Carl left us alone at the house. I think Carl may have been playing match-maker, but it didn't work. Trent is a sweetheart, and he's very much into you. He didn't ask a single question about Earl. Carl said Trent told his boss he was off the case. Said he took himself off the case the day he arrived. And from the way he stormed out of here tonight, right after you were schmoozing Ted, it's obvious. He's into you."

Mazy didn't know whether to be happy or strap on a pair of shit wading boots, cause she'd just made a mess of it. Was Trent really off the case? He sure acted like it.

She glanced back over at Ted. He was still staring and smiling. Kendal walked up the steps to the stage with her earbuds in her ears, probably listening to an audio book on her iPhone during break. She was such a little bookworm.

And Mazy felt herself shrinking inside. She'd behaved like a middle schooler. There was no way Trent would ever want to be around her again.

Mazy tossed and turned the whole night, until she finally gave up just before sunrise and threw on her bathing suit and a big T-shirt. An early morning swim usually helped her clear her head.

With a towel and a bottle of sunscreen tucked under her arm, she headed toward the beach, taking the short cut through the farm.

She gazed up at the cottage where Trent was staying and her chest tightened. She owed him an explanation, an apology, something. What could she say? "I knew that guy had a thing for me, and I flirted with him unmercifully just to make you jealous." Admit that she'd toyed with his emotions as well as Ted's? That certainly wouldn't make Trent like her any better.

She put her head down and kept walking, but the voice deep inside her wouldn't shut up. "Go talk to him." It kept repeating that mantra until she changed direction and found herself approaching the cottage. What was she going to say? Would he slam the door in her face? What if he was still asleep? Maybe she should come back later.

Still that inner voice gnawed and urged her onto the porch.

He was probably still asleep and would be pissed when she woke him up.

Oh well, he could be mad. He had a right to be. She knew she'd end up saying something stupid. That was her style whenever she was nervous, but she'd put on her big girl panties and say something. Own up to her childish shenanigans. Take it on the chin when he blessed her out.

The front windows were open, and a breeze blew the white lace curtains in the bedroom. The sound of Trent's voice filtered through the air.

"You want me back on Earl's case?" He paused. "Good.

Glad to hear it."

Shit! He changed his mind and was going after Earl again?

She crouched beside the house and peeped in the window. He was fully dressed and pacing in front of the bed, talking on his cellphone. "No. The farmer said I'm free to go anytime I want. I was just hanging around to...ummm...I just wanted to help him out a little longer. He's a nice man, reminds me of my grandfather." Trent laughed. "Shut up, man. I 'm serious." He sat on the edge of the bed. "Honestly, I don't think Stan can catch Squirrel." He strapped on his watch. "I haven't been trying lately. That's the difference."

Mazy couldn't believe her ears. Trent was arranging to be put back on Earl's case! Had she just screwed things up for Earl too? Screwing herself over was bad enough. And Trent was leaving? She left the porch and ducked around to the side of the house and squatted behind an oleander, peering through the foliage and into the side bedroom window.

Trent sat on the edge of the bed. "You think you can bring me my Harley? I'd appreciate it." He stood and walked toward the living room. "That'll be fine. It'll give me a chance to settle a few things around here first. Tie up some loose ends."

Shit. Double shit. She sat in the dirt and put her head on her knees. The front door creaked, and she sprung to her feet and bolted for the back gate, before Trent discovered her.

Mazy ran straight for the ocean until she had to stop to catch her breath, legs trembling. Gasping for air, her side hurt as if she'd just run a marathon. Once her panting eased a bit, she trudged over the dunes, willing her tired legs to climb instead of giving way and allowing her to collapse. If she did that, she'd most likely end up sobbing like a baby, and crying was never the answer.

Gritting her teeth, she groaned, and pushed forward until she reached a flat surface of firm, wet sand, covered in broken seashells. She tossed her towel onto the ground and removed her flip-flops and T-shirt. The shell shards poked her tender soles, and she grimaced as she stepped lightly and made her way to the water's edge.

The waves were white capping and a dark patch of water ran parallel to the shore, about twenty feet from the breakers. Probably a riptide, which meant being careful. In her sleep-deprived state it could pull her to her watery grave in a flash, but she was determined to swim and clear her head.

The sea always soothed her, made everything right with the world. That ocean had mended her battered heart many times. It had a way of cradling her when she needed it most, like when her mother had died, when Earl had been locked away, and when her father had left her and Earl alone to fend for themselves because they were eighteen he said, old enough to stand on their own two feet.

Now, because of her stupid idea to make him jealous, Trent was back on the case and going to hunt Earl down, Kendal was going to be crushed by her flirtatious actions with Ted, and Ted was going to get his hopes up when she had no intentions of dating him. The whole thing was a mess. She was a mess. And the very real possibility that she'd end up all alone, no family at her side, and some of her closest friends hurt and disappointed because of her was bad enough, but she'd blown it with the only man who'd ever made her feel like she could be her whole self.

Well, she was her whole self now. And it wasn't a pretty sight.

The breakers crashed around her thighs as the sand

washed away beneath her feet. She dug her toes into the soft silt and leaned into the foaming water, holding her breath as the powerful Atlantic crashed into her chest and splashed across her face. Three more long, strong strides, and she dove into an oncoming wave, swimming downward as the crest skimmed the surface.

All was quiet in her head, submerged in the saltwater, weightless. In that moment, she felt transported into another world. She wasn't ready to pop back up. Instead she kicked hard and used all the strength she had in her arms to pull herself through the water, hovering inches from the ocean's bottom, careful not to swim out too far.

The need for oxygen forced her to resurface. She put her feet down and stood, the water was barely chest high. She eased herself backward, letting her arms glide across the foam as she watched seagulls circle overhead.

Something zapped her right calf. A sharp pain shot through her leg. She turned and saw a jellyfish floating by. The excruciating pain caused a torrent of nausea to wash over her. Trying not to churn the water and draw the jellyfish toward her, she froze.

With her back to the waves, she was unprepared for the giant one that knocked her off her feet and sent her tumbling along the ocean floor, sharp shells ripping into her flesh.

She gasped and tried to stand, only to be bulldozed by another wave larger than the one before. Water went up her nose. She came up sputtering and coughing, the current pulling her out to sea.

Her stung leg wasn't cooperating. She couldn't touch bottom. The current was too strong. Her arms couldn't fight against the raging sea. She tried to scream, but another wave hit her.

Remembering what her mother taught her, she stopped

trying to fight the current and swam with it instead, gulping air every chance she had. She said a silent prayer. "Mama, if you're watching over me, please, help me. I need your help, Mama. Please."

Her arms were working too hard keeping her afloat to wave. She couldn't see the shore. She focused on the sky, air, air.

Saltwater flooded her mouth and nose. She spat and coughed, blew through her nostrils, determined to not allow water into her lungs. She kept kicking, kept swimming, adrenaline coursing through her system, giving her a surge of strength.

That strength was no match for the vicious current that yanked her under once more. She held her breath, the sun dimming as the angry sea pulled her deeper.

All her focus was on her breath, as she exhaled in teeny tiny spurts. If she could reach the bottom maybe then she could push off the ocean floor with enough force to catapult her to the surface again.

Focus. Don't panic. Conserve your energy. Prepare.

"Mama. Please. Help me."

CHAPTER ELEVEN
Mama

When Mazy reached the ocean floor, she bent her knees and pushed with all her might. She broke the surface and exhaled, and then immediately inhaled quickly, taking in as much air as possible before the fierce current forced her head back under water.

Something latched onto her injured leg. The pain from the jellyfish sting and the pressure of whatever had her in a vice grip was unbearable. God, was something biting her? Was she going to be eaten alive?

Another strong, clenching sensation encased her right forearm. She couldn't see clearly underwater. A warm body pressed against her, and a hard, muscular arm supported her back.

Thank God. Someone had found her. She knew to relax, not fight, let this person take control, be weightless in their grasp.

She was shoved toward the sky, and her head emerged. Alternating between coughing and gulping air, with her back to her rescuer, she felt like a rag doll as this person--she assumed to be a man based on the size of the arms supporting her--pulled her toward the shore.

"Mazy, I got you. Stay calm. Breathe." Trent's warm breath fell upon her ear, his voice rumbling.

She whispered, "Trent," on an exhale and clasped his arm, her fear subsiding as they neared the shore.

Through tears, she gazed up at the clouds, as one in particular seemed to form the shape of an angel. In her mind, she spoke to her mother as she'd done so many times through the years. "Thank you, Mama. Thank you for sending him to save me."

Once out of the water, Trent rolled her onto her side, and she expelled the seawater she'd inadvertently swallowed, her abdominal muscles contracting. Heaves, and ragged gurgling inhalations racked her body. Her vision blurred as tiny dark spots flickered before her eyes.

Eventually the tightness in her chest dissipated, and her breathing became steady. She closed her eyes and concentrated on the glorious feeling of air in, air out, earth beneath her. Trent's warm palm caressed her back in soothing strokes.

"There, Baby. Breathe. That's it." His voice was quiet.

Her eyes fluttered opened, and she looked up into his handsome face, his brow etched with worry lines, water dripping from his hair down his crooked nose.

He brushed the hair from her face. "I'm here." He placed his hand in hers and squeezed.

Tears filled her eyes once more, making the sight of him a fuzzy image again. She blinked and big, hot teardrops rolled down her cheeks as she shivered uncontrollably.

He leaned down and kissed her forehead, shielding her body from the wind with his broad shoulders, his warmth radiating through her. He whispered. "I need to get you warm, Mazy. I'm going to pick you up, okay?"

She nodded and wrapped her arms around his neck as he lifted her off the ground. She curled against him and clung for dear life. Her throat hurt so badly she didn't speak. Her leg burned and throbbed, but she didn't even care to mention it. All she wanted to do was breathe, in the safety of his arms.

Trent held Mazy's slender, trembling body close. When he'd first gone for a walk on the beach after getting a text from Carl telling him to enjoy his day, that he'd gone fishing with Myrtle, he'd headed to the pier, but an indescribable feeling in the pit of his stomach made him turn around and go the other direction. Then he spotted someone caught in the riptide, he had no idea it was Mazy. As he neared and saw her red hair, he'd panicked.

He'd lost sight of her when she went under. His world crashed in on him, leaving him helpless, desperate, just like when he'd lost his teammates on their last mission.

He didn't know how he found the strength to fight this riptide. His SEAL training helped, but even so, this current was beyond anything he should have been able to combat. It was as if some otherworldly force had been coursing through his veins. A force stronger than a standard adrenaline rush.

He'd been determined to find Mazy. And when her beautiful face popped to the surface, his heart leapt.

What had she been thinking, going into the water today? Thank God he'd found her.

Later, he could ask her why she was out there. Right now, he needed to get her dry and warmed up, keep her from going into shock.

Climbing the dunes with Mazy in his arms, he was thankful to be able to hold her, hear her softly breathing in his ear. She wrapped her arms around him tighter, her head on his shoulder. He squeezed her closer to him, and whispered, "Everything's going to be all right, baby. I got you."

"Thank you." Her voice was frail and filled with emotion.

He kissed the top of her head, and carried her back to the cottage.

Once inside, he eased her onto the bed, she let go of his neck and relaxed. He cupped her head and lowered it to the pillow.

He scanned her body, searching for injury. "Are you hurt anywhere?"

"A jellyfish stung my right leg. It hurts pretty bad." Her voice was brittle and her brows pleated.

"Mazy...why didn't you tell me?" He searched her leg.

When he saw the welts on her leg, he sucked in a breath with a hiss. Damn, that had to hurt.

"I just did?" She offered him a weak smile.

He stood, scratched his head and looked around. What did he have to alleviate her discomfort? He covered her with a quilt and darted out of the room to check the kitchen cupboards.

Moments later, he came back to the bedroom with a clean cloth and a bottle of white vinegar. He sat beside her and moved the quilt away from her injury.

He sat the vinegar on the nightstand, grabbed his wallet, and removed a credit card to scrape her skin to dislodge any remaining stingers. He didn't see any, but it was best to make sure. As he lightly scraped the raised streaks along her calf, she flinched. "Did I hurt you?"

"It's okay." She clenched the quilt and folded her lips inward.

"Almost done. Hang in there." When he sat the credit card aside, she blew out a breath and watched him intently. He doused the cloth with vinegar then gently patted her leg with it, squeezing the fabric so that the liquid ran over the inflamed area. He knew the sting wouldn't immediately go away, but it would, hopefully, ease off.

The bitter tang of vinegar filled his nostrils, and he could almost taste the sourness. Mazy wrinkled her nose and made a face of disgust at the odor.

He smiled. "Not a fan, huh?"

She shook her head then rested back onto the pillows and closed her eyes. She had to be exhausted.

Once he'd smoothed the wet rag over her calf, he wrapped a thick towel around the cloth and placed her leg on a pillow to elevate it.

He dug around in the closet and pulled out a heavy wool blanket, folded it in half, and draped it over her, tucking it around her body.

She smiled up at him, her sleepy eyes fluttering closed.

"Rest, sweetheart. I'll make you some hot tea. Are you hungry?"

She didn't respond. Her face muscles slackened and her breathing became slow and steady. She looked so peaceful. Trent caressed her cheek, not wanting to leave her side.

Mazy awoke drenched in sweat. She kicked the covers off of her and sat up on the side of the bed. Disoriented, she scanned the room as the fog cleared in her brain, and she got her bearings.

Memories of her near drowning replayed in her mind, eliciting a tremor of fear that ran down her spine. She clenched the sheet, as her heartbeat accelerated.

Flashes from earlier came into focus. Trent's worried face had hovered over her, and she'd sensed the presence of her mother all around her. Parts of the events seemed like a dream more than reality, as if they'd happened to someone else.

The taste of saltwater was still on her tongue, and her hair was crunchy, clumps of sand embedded in her curls. A dull throb in her leg confirmed that none of what she'd recalled was a dream, it'd been real, and she'd survived. Thanks to Trent and her guardian angel.

Male voices came from the other room. Trent's voice and the voice of a man with a Bostonian accent.

She pushed to her feet and limped to the door. Crouching, she peered through the keyhole and listened in. Eavesdropping seemed to be her favorite thing to do these days where Trent was concerned. But without knowing who that man was, she thought it'd best not to make her presence known.

Squinting with her nose pressed to the door, she looked through the large, old-fashioned keyhole.

Trent was talking to some lanky guy, mid-fifties, dark hair.

The stranger said, "I sure wish you'd reconsider going back on the Washington case, I don't have much faith in Stan for this one."

Trent patted the guy's shoulder. "Sorry, man. I'm done being a runner. I'm in the market for a new line of work. Hopefully, I'll find something around here. I like this place."

Mazy smiled so hard her cheeks hurt. Trent wasn't on Earl's case, and he was planning on staying on the island. This was HUGE.

Yuck. The stench of vinegar was making her sick to her stomach, not to mention her own stench from sweating like a horse rode hard because of all the blankets piled on top of her while she napped .

She saw a few T-shirts and a stack of sweatpants folded on a shelf in the closet. She helped herself and stepped into the bathroom for a quick shower.

Trent unloaded his motorcycle from Jimmy's trailer and bid the man farewell. When he came back inside the cottage, he heard the shower running and smiled. Good. Mazy was up. And she'd probably be hungry.

He went into the kitchen and warmed some of the chili he'd made the day before. Chili was always better the second day anyway.

When Mazy entered the living room, he had to catch his breath. The sight of her in a white T-shirt with her wet hair dripping over her breasts, her hardened nipples soaked and visible, made him want to clear off the kitchen table and take her right there.

He couldn't help but stare. God. There she was--scrubbed clean, comfy, sexy, soft. He had to fight the urge to rush to her side and kiss her from head to toe.

She smiled at him, and he shivered. Back to reality. *Say something.* "Hey there, Sleeping Beauty. Come have a seat at the table. I'm warming up some chili. You've gotta be hungry."

She rubbed her tummy. "I'm starving."

He ladled a healthy serving into a bowl and placed it in front of her.

She reached up and took his hand in hers and pressed her lips to his knuckles. Chin lifted and a smile on her lips, she wrapped her arms around his hips and drew him close, then buried her face in his stomach.

She turned her head to the side and whispered, "I owe you my life. I don't even know how to begin to say thank you for rescuing me today."

He stroked her hair gently, not knowing what to say. Here she was thanking him, and he was feeling grateful to be near her. If he hadn't been able to pull her to safety today, if she'd drowned right in front of him? He squeezed his eyes shut at the thought.

Pulling free from her grasp, he made eye contact with her then knelt by her side.

Gazing into her blue/green hazel eyes that were now the color of the Caribbean sea, he said, "Thank you for fighting to stay alive. I know we've only known each other a short while, but..." When it happened he didn't know, but he loved her. She captured his heart the first day they'd met, and the more he'd gotten to know her, the more he wanted to know. He wanted to know everything about her. That news would probably send her running, seeing as she and Ted might be an item. "But...you're someone I want in my life for a long time."

She pinched her lips into a straight line, a darkness brewing in her eyes. Had he said too much?

She threw her arms around his neck and kissed him. Guess he'd said the right thing.

Mazy floated on a dreamy cloud with Trent's lips pressed to hers, his arms enveloping her, his hot breath mixing with her own.

He pulled back and held her gaze in his. "I need to know if you and Ted--"

"I'm not interested in Ted." She blurted out.

"You seemed interested yesterday."

"I know. I was just being a flirt to get back at you for having dinner with Leah. I thought--"

"You thought I had asked Leah out?"

"Yeah. I thought...well, she's beautiful...I'm--"

"Even more beautiful." He kissed her again, and her arousal became difficult to ignore.

She squirmed out of his grip. "Last night, I acted like a middle schooler at a skating rink, flirting with one boy to make the boy she really liked jealous. I'm really sorry."

"As long as you don't really have feelings for Ted, I'm fine."

She grinned. "I heard you tell that guy you planned to stay on the island."

He brushed the hair from her face. His gray eyes flickered with passion deep within as he lowered his face to hers. "Everything I want or need is here. Why would I leave?"

Gulp. "Umm, so you aren't chasing Earl?"

He smiled. "The moment I found myself more worried about upsetting you and chose not to go through your contact list on your phone, I knew I was off Squirrel's trail."

"That happened the day you got here."

"Yep. I pulled myself off Earl's case that very evening. I tried to tell you that, but you didn't believe me."

"So, you've been here the whole time--"

"Because I wanted to be here." He pressed his lips to the corner of her smile, skimming his hot mouth across her cheek, until his lips brushed hers. "Isn't it obvious by now, you're the only one I'm interested in chasing?"

And with that little speech, he'd just caught her. She sighed.

He stood and moved the bowl closer to her. "Eat up while it's hot."

She gazed at his belt buckle, then her eyes dropped to his fly and the denim cupping him lovingly. Yeah, eat up, she needed to do that.

Trent couldn't take his eyes off Mazy as she chowed down, eating two bowls of chili back to back. Color had come back to her cheeks, and her hair had dried into copper coils. "I have some cheesecake in the fridge if you'd like some."

She beamed. "Any topping?"

"Strawberry."

"Mmm. My favorite."

He cut her a slice of cake and spooned the strawberry topping over it. When he sat the cheesecake in front of her, she looked up at him and smiled. "I'm feeling so much better. Not just physically. I mean, I'm--"

He ran a finger down her nose. "A light heart and a full belly, that's the way I want you."

She dug into the cheesecake and took a big bite. "Mmmm."

He watched her devour the dessert, loving the sounds she made enjoying it. He wanted to hear her make sounds as she enjoyed a lot of things.

Kneeling beside her as she finished the last bite, his eyes fell to her pink lips and the glistening dollop of strawberry topping at the corner of her mouth. He bowed his head to hers and licked the strawberry goodness. She turned and kissed him full on. Her mouth was sweeter and more succulent than the strawberries.

He needed to taste all of her. Every. Last. Inch. "I want you, Mazy."

CHAPTER TWELVE
Massage

Mazy quivered from the way Trent said he wanted her. His voice a low growl, like a lion crouched within him ready to pounce and devour her lick by lick.

He lit a vanilla scented candle and placed it on the night stand. With his hand on the mattress and a wicked gleam in his eye, he patted the mattress. "Here."

What could she say? She was his marionette, and he could pull her strings with a look, a gesture, a word.

She crawled onto the bed, as he opened a bottle of oil.

"All the fighting you did with that ocean today, you're going to be sore. If you let me give you a massage, it'll help."

She thought he lured her back to bed to have sex. She *wanted* to have sex with him. He just wanted to give her a massage? She tried not to let the disappointment show on her face. This was awkward. Okay, well, fine. Maybe he's not the kind to rush into things. She did feel a little tightness in her neck and upper shoulders. She lied on her stomach, with her hands folded beneath her chin, her head turned so she could see him.

He quirked an eyebrow. "Works better if you take the shirt off."

Oh, so he was being naughty. All right then. She rose to her knees and tugged her shirt off and tossed it aside. He warmed some oil between his palms, desire in his heated gaze as he scanned her body with a hungry expression.

Feeling mischievous, she tucked her thumbs into the waistband of her sweatpants. His mouth opened and his breathing became shallow. As she slid her pants off, revealing the fact she had nothing on beneath them, he rubbed his hands together faster, and an impressive erection swelled in his jeans.

After seeing him naked on Bare Point and placing her life in his hands today, screw being bashful. Bring it on.

On her hands and knees, she arched and spread her legs, letting him see everything, loving the way his face showed her how much he was enjoying the view.

She whispered, "I'd feel more comfortable if you were naked too."

He moved closer to the edge of the bed. "My hands are all greasy. Maybe you could help me out."

Gladly. She crawled toward him and bit the edge of his T-shirt and lifted her head, bringing the fabric up with her as she sat back and slid her hands under the shirt, pushing it toward his shoulders. Smooth, taut, sun-kissed skin shimmered beneath the pads of her fingers. Running her palm over his rippling six-pack abs, he made a manly sound of approval in the back of his throat. She leaned forward and kissed him over each hardened muscle along his torso, all the way up to the center of his chest. His masculine, clean scent made her want more. Gently nibbling his pecs, licking lightly over his nipples, she pushed the shirt higher as he yanked his head free from the collar.

This. All this hard muscle was hers for the taking. Mmm. He was beautiful.

Her eyes found his and the message they were sending was more loving than she'd expected. She'd anticipated passion in his gaze, but not the tenderness that accompanied it. She rose to kiss him, and he leaned down, meeting her halfway.

"You're so damn sexy, Mazy." He spoke the words softly into her opened mouth then sealed their lips with a slow kiss that left them both trembling.

God, he was the sexy one.

Blindly feeling for his belt buckle, she found it and opened it, unbuttoned his jeans, unzipped his fly. His erection sprang out toward her, long, thick, hard. She grasped the shaft and looked down at his gorgeous cock, crown glistening. She could feel his pulse beneath her fingers, reminding her, this wasn't just a cock, this was a part of him. And she wanted all of Trent McAllister.

He stepped back and his jeans fell to the floor. She still held him firmly in her grip and began to gently stroke him up and down, trailing over that wet tip, slicking her palm with his pre-cum so her hand glided more easily.

He gritted his teeth and pushed his pelvis toward her, watching her with intensity, but not touching her.

"That's it." She cooed. "Mmm. Let me have it. Mine?" She flashed a grin, knowing damn well that hardened cock was hers right now.

"Fuck." He groaned through his teeth. "Yes. Yours, baby." His thigh muscles flexed, and he rocked his pelvis, causing his stomach to ripple and his shaft to pump in her fist.

She needed to taste him. Lowering her head, she gazed into his eyes and slipped him into her mouth. He grabbed a handful of her hair and guided her up and down slowly.

"Mazy...I...Oh fu..." His head fell back, and he clenched her hair tighter.

She increased speed, which made him even harder.

His arousal was making her wet.

He pulled himself away from her and blew out a breath, his eyes closed, fists at his side. "Not yet, baby. Damn, you make me want to--"

"Come," she whispered.

He folded his lips inward and nodded then swallowed loudly as she watched his Adam's apple bob, and his chest rise and fall with deep breaths.

He picked up the oil again and said, "There's no hurry here, Mazy. Lie on your stomach for me."

He wasn't going to let her finish what she'd started? Really? Okay...taking it slow. Fine.

She stretched out and pulled her hair to the side, as she watched him crawl onto the bed beside her. She was tempted to reach out and stroke him again, but hey, if he wanted to slow down with that, maybe she should just let him lead the way.

When his slick hands pressed and rubbed from her lower back to her neck, she melted. "Oh God...I didn't know it would feel so good."

He kneaded his thumbs into the knotted muscles at the base of her skull and her eyes rolled back. "Mmm." When the scent of coconut from the oil filled her nose, she repeated the "Mmm."

Pushing with his palms, he made his way down her spine, one by one her vertebrae popped back in place beneath the pressure he applied. So good. Earl used to crack her back for her sometimes, but never like this. This was way better. Wow.

Heck, maybe this *was* better than sex.

Trent's strong hands worked every inch of her back then he spread her legs and crawled between them. Grabbing her hips he raised them and whispered, "Hold it right there."

She kept her bottom arched toward him, and he slipped a pillow beneath her. She rested back down, open and wet.

He squirted some more oil in his hands and placed a palm on each of her thighs, then kneaded and massaged from the back of her knees to her bottom. As he neared her groin his thumbs grazed her lips.

Yes. There. Please.

His mouth almost touching her ear. "Do you want me, Mazy?"

"Yes." She whimpered.

"I don't want a sampling. I don't want a fuck. I want you to give yourself to me and let me make you come, be your man. Can you give yourself to me, Mazy?" He brushed an oily thumb over her clit. Her nipples hardened.

"Yessss."

"That's my girl." He rubbed her ass in slow circles, a palm on each cheek. Spreading her open, the breeze from the ceiling fan tickling over her moistened folds.

He kept his hands roving, massaging, finding her butt muscles and pushing, rubbing. It felt like he'd poked a bruise, but it didn't hurt, it was an exquisite kind of sore feeling. As he neared her tailbone he said, "Are you still in any kind of pain from that fall."

"No. I'm in no pain." What she was feeling was the opposite of pain.

"Good. No pain for my girl, only pleasure. Do you like to be pleasured?"

"Yes." Dear God. He was going to make her come just from the questions he was asking.

He ran an oily thumb over her clit.

She gasped.

"Yes. You like to be pleasured."

"Oh. Please."

His thumb stroked her slowly. "Like this?"

"Ahhh. Yessss."

He moved his hand away and her brow furrowed. Noooo. He needed to keep doing that.

She must have been whimpering, cause he said, "Shhh. I'll come back to that puffy little clit."

He squeezed her ass in his hands and kissed her at the top of her crack and feathered his tongue up her spine to her waist. As he leaned over her his cock rested on her bottom, tickling over her skin.

He rocked back on his heels and gripped his shaft then rubbed his tip over her wetness, cleaving her moist lips open, until the head of his cock made contact with her swollen, sensitive nub.

She clenched the sheets and arched.

He leaned over her and whispered in her ear, "I think I found the spot that really needs massaging." He ground his hips.

Her eyes fluttered closed.

"My sexy woman. I almost lost you today, lost you before I'd even had the chance to show you how much I want you." He rubbed her faster. "Is it okay that I want you, Mazy?"

Jesus. He had to ask? All she could do was moan.

"I've wanted you since the first day I saw you. Did you know I saw *her* that day?" He slid a finger inside her entrance and wiggled it.

"Oh fuck."

"Yeah. I saw *her*, and I wanted *her* all to myself." He pumped another finger inside and she could hear her slickness, the sexy wet clicking.

"Take *her*." She couldn't think anymore.

He leaned down and kissed her neck. "Turn over for me."

He moved back, and she did as instructed, the pillow beneath her bottom, forcing her pelvis toward the ceiling. He kissed her long and deep, his hands now on her breasts, tugging her nipples into tight beads.

With his mouth on hers, he reached to the nightstand and opened the drawer. He retrieved something, but she didn't know what.

As he sat back on his heels again, he placed a thumb on each side of her entrance and stroked with firm pressure that caused her clit to protrude. He held the oil bottle up in the air and let the clear fluid drizzle onto her sensitive, pink bud, blooming between her folds.

The oil trickled over her and down her crack. Trent grabbed her behind the knees and lifted them, spreading them wider, then placed a palm against her entire mound.

She couldn't help but to grind against his hand as he pressed in circular motions.

Squeezing her own breasts, she lifted her head and looked down at what he was doing. He pushed her feminine lips together, trapping her excited clit between them, then rocked his hand side to side. Oh God, he'd found the root of her pleasure point. She trembled and lifted her hips toward him. Holding her taut in his fingers, he ran the thumb of his other hand over her exposed hood, gently, barely touching.

"Ahhh." She couldn't hold it in. She cried out and closed her eyes.

"Does that feel good?"

"Yessss."

He added more pressure and rubbed faster, releasing her lips and sliding a finger into her, curling upward against her inner wall.

She couldn't think. Her body tensed and contracted. He didn't stop, he rode it out with her, keeping his movements precisely how she needed them inside and out, until she was thrashing and bucking. An orgasm ripped through her body. She didn't know what she was saying, but she heard herself crying out with release.

Never had she ever felt like this. God.

Trembling, panting, riding the after waves, he slid himself inside her. She lifted her head to watch. He had a condom wrapper in his hand and his cock was sheathed in latex. When did he do this? Thank God one of them still had their wits about them.

He stretched her open with a deep thrust, then held still as her inner muscles relaxed to adjust to his girth.

Staring into her eyes, he said. "Now. Look at me. *Really* look at me. See yourself in my eyes. You're so fucking beautiful." He pushed himself in and out of her slowly.

His eyes held affection, passion, and something else,

something she'd never witnessed, something so strong it made her feel exposed to the bone.

She reached for him. He positioned himself on top of her, leaning on his elbows, his face hovering above hers.

Her hips rested on the pillow, angling her just right.

He whispered, "Give yourself to me." Then he claimed her mouth with his, his tongue mimicking his thrusts below. She wrapped her arms and legs around him, wanting all of him.

Lost in his kiss and the way he made love to her, she felt another orgasm well within her.

He tore himself away from her mouth and studied her face, as he pumped harder, faster, his eyes never leaving hers.

He grabbed her wrist and guided her hand between her legs. "Rub her for me. Rub fast and good."

She did.

He smiled and thrust harder. "Come for me."

Her body was so obedient. Ooo. Her canal muscles spasmed around him, as an orgasm quaked within.

He groaned and shuddered, releasing into her.

So this was what it was supposed to be like.

Holy Shit.

She'd never felt so fulfilled before, so content, so loved. He made her feel *loved*.

She placed her hands on each side of his face as their breathing calmed and the waves of passion subsided. "No one has ever made love to me like that before."

He kissed her deeply. "Then no one has ever loved you before. Until now."

Trent watched Mazy sleep in his arms. Making love to her had been the most moving experience in his life. Never had he felt such emotion, such connection with anyone, including his ex wife. He'd heard when you met the right person for you, you'd know, but he thought that was just an old cliché everyone said, like "everything happens for a reason." But there was something to those sayings. He sensed strongly that a higher power had brought him to Pleasure Island, and led him out onto that beach when Mazy almost drowned. Having only known Mazy mere days, he knew without a doubt she was the one for him.

Rushing into things wasn't a good idea. It'd all blown up in his face the first time he'd taken his vows and walked down the aisle. No, this time, if the road was leading to matrimony, he'd welcome it, but he wasn't going to run toward it. If Mazy was the girl for him, they had time, time enough to really get to know each other properly. There were so many things he had yet to learn about her, and he wanted to learn everything, every last detail of her past, her pet peeves, her dreams and ambitions.

Mazy stirred, her eyes opened slowly as she stretched and yawned. She looked up at him and smiled. "What time is it?"

He glanced at the digital bedside clock. "Six fifteen."

It was still light outside. The long days of summer were upon them. It wouldn't start getting dark for another two to three hours.

She sat up quickly. "Oh no." Her eyes were wide with panic.

"What's wrong? Did you have a gig tonight? I thought it was Bingo night at Reel to Real Good."

"It is Bingo night. No, I didn't have a gig. I haven't fed Rooster all day. He's probably sitting in his pen crying, thinking I don't love him anymore."

He couldn't help but smile at the way she described Rooster, how fond she was of him.

She stood and got dressed in a flash. He was disappointed to see her luscious body be covered up in baggy clothes.

She looked over at him. "Hurry up. Let's go."

She wanted him to come with her? Excellent. He grinned. "Yes, Ma'am. You know, when you get a little bossy, it's a turn on."

She slapped his arm and laughed.

He stood, his back to her. She smacked his butt, left it stinging. He bent over. "Please, Ma'am, may I have another?"

"Oh my God. You're kinky, aren't you?"

He laughed. He'd never been into being dominated or being the one dominating. He was just joking around with her, but hearing her say *kinky* got his blood going. He faced her, letting her get a good look at just how much he was enjoying where this conversation was headed. "I'm whatever you want me to be. As long as it's just you and me, and you're getting off."

Her mouth fell open.

He laughed and pulled on a pair of sweats that tented over his erection.

"What about you?" Her voice crackled.

"About me? You mean is it important that I get off too?"

"Yeah."

He slipped on a T-shirt. "Babe, you need to know something right now. I get off on seeing you, hearing you, tasting you, and feeling you come."

"You can have an orgasm just watching me have one?"

"Well, I might help it along a little, but, yes, pretty much."

She was still as a statue.

"Let's go feed Rooster." He popped her on the butt.

She shook her head like she was jarred back to reality. "Rooster? Oh shit, Rooster. Right. Let's go." Her gaze fell to his crotch. "Can you walk like that?"

He burst out laughing, which helped his condition, slightly. "I'll be fine. It'll go down as soon as we change the subject."

She smiled. "I'll try not to say anything then. Cause, I'm kind of one track minded right now." She made big eyes at his tented pants.

"That makes two of us."

CHAPTER THIRTEEN
Challenge

Mazy unlatched Rooster's pen, and he trotted over to her, oinking to beat the band. "Hey there, buddy. I'm sorry I forgot you today. Here you go." She poured some food into his feeding bin, happy to see he still had plenty of water. As she watched him eat, Trent walked toward the creek out back.

Once she'd given Rooster some cuddling, and he had a belly full, she set out to join Trent. She found him sitting on a rock at the edge of the waterfall.

"Hey. Nice out here, isn't it?"

He faced her and said, "Yeah. I like it, quiet, peaceful. I noticed you've been planting some flower beds in this area and have cleared a good section of the land. You planning on building something back here or planting a garden?"

She perched on the rock beside him. "I've been saving up so I can build my dream home--a brick house with a big kitchen and a breakfast nook overlooking the creek. I also want it to have a large family room that leads to a screened-in back porch with a view of the waterfall. I have the blueprints picked out, as well as all the materials and finishes. I hope to be able to get the foundation put in early fall."

His expression told her he was a bit surprised, but impressed. "So, are you thinking a ranch style home?"

"Those are nice, but I prefer the houses with a higher pitched roof. I was hoping to build a jam room upstairs, pad the walls to keep the noise down, get an extra drumset so I can leave one upstairs and never have to move it. Same thing with a small sound system. My friend Kendal said she has an old electric piano she'd give me. That way when she comes over, she'll have something already in place too."

"You've given this a lot of thought."

Boy had she. She'd obsessed over it for years. She could hardly believe she was so close to making it happen. "It's a big deal for me. This was my mother's land. Mine now, but it was passed down generation to generation in her family. Five acres. Her grandfather got it dirt cheap, but it's worth a pretty penny now. She wanted me to make sure Dad and Earl always had a home to come back to. But this old trailer is on its last leg, and I don't see any sense in just getting another trailer. They depreciate too much. I want a real home, you know?"

He reached out and took her hand in his. "I do know. You'll have to show me your blueprints, swatches, sketches, whatever you got."

She smiled. "I bet this is boring to you."

He wrapped his arm around her. "Sitting here with you, getting a glimpse into your dreams, this is far from boring to me. This is the good stuff." He pulled her close and planted a kiss on her forehead.

He was right. This was the good stuff.

Trent followed Mazy into her trailer, eyeing her round rump the whole time.

She walked over to the bookcase and looked through her CD collection. "Sorry this isn't much of a living room. Earl and I had to sell off all our furniture to pay bills after Mom died, and I never got around to refurnishing the place properly. Besides, I like having the open room for my drums anyway. It's easier to bring them in and out without having to dodge tables and chairs."

She loaded a CD and pushed play. The familiar riff from "Let's Stay Together" filled the air. She sang along with Al Green. "I'm...I'm so in love with you...whatever you want to do...is alright with me... cause you make me feel so brand new."

He joined in. "And I...want to spend my life with you...."

Pulling her into his arms, they sang to each other and danced, one song after another. He didn't want this moment of pure joy to end.

Her head rested on his chest. They swayed as the music shifted into a slow song.

She looked up at him. "I've never slow danced in my own living room before."

He squeezed her tighter. "Anything you've never done before, and you'd like to try, let me know. I'm your man."

She smiled. "I'll keep that in mind."

He dipped her, and her hair touched the floor. With his face inches from hers, he said, "I've got plenty of moves to show you that I bet you've never seen before."

Giggling as he pulled her up and gave her a spin, she said, "You're a good dancer."

Fingers entwined, rocking side to side, face to face, heart to heart, he bent his head and kissed her tenderly.

As he pulled away, she sighed and said, "And you're a *great* kisser."

"Are you always this sweet?" The day they'd met, he liked her right off, but he'd pegged her to be a bit rougher, not nearly so soft and loving.

She laughed. "You're the first person to ever call me sweet. I'm a lot of things, but...I don't know...I'm different with you."

"Do I bring out the sweetness in you?" He lowered his head for another taste of her mouth.

She whispered, "You bring out a side of me I've never known."

"Let it out, baby. I love every side you have."

When she lifted her chin and kissed him this time, the passion between them was more intense. He scooped her up into his arms and she wrapped her legs around him as they explored each other's mouth with their tongues, exchanging moans, and sharing air. He supported her with his hands cradling her bottom.

Her cellphone chirped. She pulled back, wide-eyed, and he lowered her so she could stand.

She darted to the kitchen and grabbed her phone from the charger on the counter. "Oh no. I've missed eleven calls today! I've been so out of it." She placed the phone to her ear and turned her back to him. "Hello." She glanced at him then walked down the hall.

He didn't know who she was talking to, but he hoped it wasn't Ted. Maybe it was her brother.

His stomach tightened. Jimmy told him earlier that the charges against Earl had just been raised from larceny to murder. Maybe he should have mentioned that to Mazy when he found out, but something about seeing her stroll into the kitchen in a wet T-shirt completely rattled his brain. He'd been putty in her hands ever since, and Earl, or anyone else for that matter, never entered his thoughts.

When she returned to the kitchen, her face was etched with worry. He could feel her tension from ten feet away. He walked over to her. "Anything wrong?"

She shook her head.

"You sure?"

She started to put down her phone then looked up at him, and put it behind her back.

"Mazy, was that Earl?"

She stared down at the floor.

"Did he tell you the charges against him have been increased?"

Her chin shot up. "How'd you know that?"

"Jimmy told me today."

She scowled. "Why did he tell you that? Was he trying to get some information about Earl out of you?"

"He wanted me back on the case. I told him no. I

thought you knew that."

Tears welled in her eyes. "I did. I just wanted you to say it again, so I could be sure I hadn't dreamt it."

"Hey, what's going on here?" He kept his voice quiet as he drew her into his arms. "Talk to me."

"Some guy, I don't remember his name, some drug dealer was shot, and someone's trying to pin it on Earl." She trembled against him. Tears streamed down her cheeks. "They're so stupid. I mean...Earl is terrified of guns, ever since he and Dad went hunting and he accidentally shot Dad. The bullet only grazed his ear, but still, it scared Earl so bad he won't go near a gun to this day."

A killer afraid of guns? This news got Trent's wheels spinning. Earl was accused of shooting Vic Barton, a well-known cocaine dealer on the coast of South Carolina. Vic had a lot of enemies, high profile enemies at that. Maybe Squirrel *was* being set up. "Did Earl mention a friend, someone tipping him off?"

She backed away. "Why? Suddenly you're interested in the case? What? Is there more money in it for you if he's wanted for murder?"

"Don't be ridiculous. I'm on your side. Whether you believe me or not is your choice. Doesn't change facts though. I have no interest in hunting your brother down and turning him over to the police. As a matter of fact, I'm breaking the rules to be here. I can't go back to that line of work again. Are you kidding me? If Jimmy knew you and I were hooking up, he'd throw the book at me."

"You could get in trouble for being with me?" The concern in her voice tore at his heart.

"I'm not getting into trouble, sweetheart. I'm sending in my resignation to make it official. There's nothing Jimmy can do to me." He wasn't sure that was a hundred percent true, since technically, he was messing around with a family member of the man he'd been hired to hunt down before he'd made his resignation as a runner official. Yeah. He'd pulled himself off the case, however, he hadn't quit his job in writing. But he didn't want to think about that right now.

"Then why are you asking about Earl now?"

"Cause he's your family, and you love him. I was hoping maybe I could help you. It sounds like there might be some truth to his claim of being set up."

She studied his face. The way she kept switching gears, angry with him, worried about him, upset that he was asking questions, he couldn't get a read on what was going on in that head of hers.

She took a deep breath. "I'll ask him for names next time he calls. He just told me his buddy tipped him off, never gave the guy's name. He hasn't been telling me much of anything. He says the less I know, the better."

The thought of Mazy being in danger hadn't crossed his mind. And it should have. Vic Barton was bad news, and anyone associated with him was just as bad. Boy, his mind had been so preoccupied with Mazy, he'd turned stupid. Good thing Earl was smart enough to not give her any information. "He's probably right about that."

Mazy turned and sat down at the kitchen table and stared out the window.

Trent sat across from her. "Listen, he's okay now." He squeezed her hand.

She squeezed his hand back and said, "Thank you. I'm glad you're here. I'd hate to be facing this alone." Her eyes found his.

He understood the fear of being alone all too well. He'd been more alone this past year than ever and the detachment from his teammates and the loss of those he loved had made him brittle.

Mazy sensed she could trust Trent with everything, including information about Earl. She didn't understand why she felt so strongly about it, but she did, and having him by her side meant the world to her.

Sure, she had friends, lots of friends. But having a big, strong man in her corner, arms to hold her until the fear subsided was something none of her friends could give her, only him.

He got up from the table and walked to the fridge and checked out the family photos displayed on the freezer door. "Is this a picture of your mother?" He pointed to a photograph of Mazy's mother from back in the 80's. She had big hair, too much makeup and a black mini dress, hot pink pumps and little white ankle socks with a lace ruffle around the cuff.

"Yep. That was my mom back in the day." Mazy walked over to the fridge and pulled off a different picture of her mother. "This one's my favorite though. It was taken a couple of years before she passed. She loved sitting on the pier, watching the sunrise." She ran a finger over her mother's long red hair billowing in the ocean breeze, a pink sunrise filling the sky, her white sundress fluttering in the wind. "She looked so beautiful that morning, like an angel."

Trent stared at the picture and said, "I thought that was a picture of you."

This was how he saw *her*? Like *this*? She bit her quivering bottom lip. "I take that as a huge compliment."

He kissed her cheek then pointed to another photograph. "God. I can't tell you and Earl apart in this one."

She laughed when she saw the picture he was talking about. "Oh man, we used to skateboard all over town when we were in middle school. Louise even called the sheriff on us when we were doing tricks off her deck. She was scared we were going to break our necks."

He moved in close to a picture of her sitting on her dirt bike, wearing a helmet, and holding the championship trophy she'd won. "Earl's always loved to ride bikes, I see."

"That's me."

"You?"

"Yep. I beat Earl's time by ten seconds. He came in third. A guy from Garner came in second."

He pulled the picture off the fridge and scrutinized it, then smiled. "So tell me something...the first day we met...when I chased Earl onto the farm...was that you?"

She giggled. "Yep."

He threw his head back and laughed. "I can hear the taunts from the townfolk now. He thought he was chasing Squirrel, but it wasn't Earl, it was a girl." He scrubbed a hand down his face. "Mazy, please tell me folks don't already know about this."

"They know."

"Oh good. I mean...they need something to gnaw on besides my fried frank."

She playfully punched him in the arm. "You've been giving them loads to gnaw on since you got here. They just had a little snack at the wienie roast."

He cocked his head and gave her the evil eye. "Little snack?"

She laughed.

"Little snack, Mazy?"

"Oh my God!" She laughed harder.

"Oh my God size. Yeah. That's what I thought."

"It's quite a mouthful." She grinned.

He just smiled and raised his brows.

She wiped her eyes with her the back of her hand. "You could use a few driving lessons...just saying."

"You think so, huh? Well, Little Miss Hot Rod, Jimmy

brought me my bike today, so anytime you want to give me a few lessons, we can go for a ride."

"When I get in the mood for a ride. I'll let you know." She licked her lips.

He snatched her to his chest, looked down into her eyes, and said, "Don't tease me. I know how to make you beg for a ride."

All her excited little nerve endings went Whee all the way down the slide at the playground between her thighs. "Prove it."

Trent grinned. "Challenge accepted."

CHAPTER FOURTEEN
Pizza

Trent gathered Mazy's hair and lifted it from her neck. Her skin glistened like a dew-kissed gardenia. The moonlight streamed through the blinds.

Sitting, face to face, with her legs around him, his cock was still inside her. Her inner walls spasmed around his shaft, as the final tremors of release rippled through her.

The breeze from the ceiling fan caused the curls about her face to dance. Her eyes were closed, her lips parted, and she sighed as if a bird had burst free from its cage somewhere deep inside her to soar high above them.

He longed to stay like this, watching the contentment soften her features, the slackness in her muscles as she leaned against his arm wrapped around her waist, her hands resting softly upon his shoulders.

He wanted nothing more than to be the man with the privilege to hold her, and gaze upon her nakedness, a nakedness that far exceeded mere flesh. It went deeper.

In this quiet post-coital moment of connection, he realized he'd been a fool to ever think remaining detached and constantly moving was his only mode of survival, his only route to salvation. In fact, it'd been hell on earth. Braided into one with Mazy, this was sanctuary. This was where all the roads before this day had led him, and here is where he belonged.

She tilted her head to the side and smiled, eyes remaining closed. "I'm going to be so sore in the morning."

"I'll kiss it and make it better." He pressed his lips to the hollow between her breasts.

Her laugh was edged with a hum of pleasure.

As he let go of her damp locks, she touched her forehead to his, her waves of auburn hair blanketing his face.

She whispered, "Know what I want?"

"What's that?" His exhaustion, apparent in his rumbling,

muted voice.

"Pizza!" She flipped her hair back and bounced on his lap.

"God. Don't do that." He winced, his sensitive cock, thrumming with pain from her sudden movements.

"Oh, sorry." She stilled, and whispered, "Pizza?"

In the dim light, her eyes sparkled as if fairies were having a party in the forest of her green eyes.

When the white light of the sun had illuminated her frightened eyes that afternoon, her irises had appeared gray, as if thunderclouds were forming within them.

And when he'd steadied her against the kitchen counter and entered her, with the fluorescent light flickering overhead, her face flushed, her hair a crimson corona, those magical eyes of hers had been turquoise with flashes of silver.

Now, playful, and famished, the pixie within Mazy fully emerged, and he would indulge her every whim. "Pepperoni?"

"And pineapple." She sat up straight.

"I've never eaten it that way, but okay. I hear pineapple makes your juice taste sweeter. Not that you need any sweetening in that department." He squeezed her butt.

"Do I taste bad?" She furrowed her brows.

He laughed. "Oh my God. You have to ask? If I didn't like the way you taste, do you think I'd hold you down and devour you?" She quivered around him. Mmm. That comment had a nice effect. He'd be sure to partake of her sweetness again before the night was over. "You taste amazing." And with that confirmation, he licked her nipple and sucked it into his mouth.

After motor-boating her boobs briefly, eliciting a giggle from her, a giggle that reached his shaft, he lifted his head and grinned. "Large, extra large, thin crust, or deep dish?"

She rotated her hips. "Extra large, *deep* dish."

They both burst out laughing.

He made his dick twitch, and her eyes widened. He licked his lips and lifted a brow and said, "You're so cheesy."

When she giggled once more, he felt it on his cock again, but also somewhere deeper, somewhere that hadn't experienced joy in a very, very long time.

Mazy cleared off the coffee table and threw the pizza box away. "Want another beer?"

Trent, wearing black boxer briefs and nothing else, leaned back on the couch. "That'd be great. Thanks. Hey, do you have Netflix?"

"Nah. I don't watch much T.V. Just the basic cable is enough for me." She walked down the hall to fetch a couple of cold beers.

When she returned to the den, he pointed to her stash of DVD's. "I notice you like movies. Romantic comedies especially."

Oh great. Here it comes. Earl used to make fun of her for watching all those "rush to the airport to profess your love" endings. Trent was probably going to take a jab at her too.

"Sucker for a happy ending?" He asked with sincerity, no sarcasm detected.

"Guess so. I know that stuff isn't real life, but if I'm going to escape for a couple of hours by watching a movie, I want to go somewhere fun, end with my heart full and a smile on my face."

"Nothing wrong with that."

"What kinds of movies do you like, military thrillers?"

"Oh hell no. I lived that shit. I don't need to watch it on the big screen. They never get it right anyway, and it grates my nerves."

"Never get it right? What, the technical aspects of combat?"

He didn't answer. Instead, he stared off into the distance. Had she hit upon a sore spot? He was damn near catatonic now. She sat beside him and placed his beer on the coffee table in front of him.

With his eyes closed and his head back, she watched the muscles in his jaw flex as he ground his teeth, breathing deeply, his hands clenched into tight fists on his thighs.

She didn't know if she should touch him gently, ask him what was wrong, just let him work it out in his head, or flee before he had some kind of violent PTSD episode. She chose to stay put, keep her hands to herself, her mouth shut, and give him a moment.

When he opened his eyes, he stared at her. She sensed he was struggling to form his thoughts into words. So, she said, "We don't have to talk about it, if you don't want to."

He blew out a breath and nodded. "I want to talk about it." He picked up his beer and lifted it to his mouth for a long pull. "Want isn't the right word. I need to talk about it."

She drew her legs up and sat cross-legged, facing him, sipping her beer.

Placing a hand on her knee, his brows pleated, and he swallowed loudly, as if the words he held inside were burning his throat. "Mazy, I've done a lot of evil things for the right reasons, if you call serving your country a right reason. I'd prepared myself to do whatever it took, whatever orders demanded, no reservations. But nothing prepared me for the torture of not being able to do a damn thing."

She didn't understand what he meant, but remained silent, hoping he'd explain.

It took him several minutes and several more swigs of beer before he continued. "Watching my teammates die around me. Lying in a pool of blood beneath Mark, my best friend, who died after throwing himself over me...he sacrificed himself and saved my life." He paused, closed his eyes, shaking his head.

God. She couldn't imagine what that must have been like.

She caressed his forearm with her free hand. He looked at her, his gaze roving her face as if he were searching for a sign of some kind. What could she say to that? It's okay? That wouldn't help him. If it were okay, he wouldn't be so upset about it in the first place.

He offered a weak smile that didn't reach his eyes. "I remember being so proud to even be accepted into the BUD/S program to become a Navy SEAL. It was the first time I'd ever felt special, gifted. Hell, I don't know." He took another gulp from the bottle. "I served four years active duty. That's it. Four years. My last mission, I got too close to an IED, suffered brain trauma. Then boom. Medical discharge. Sent back home."

He caught his breath, his eyes foggy and distant. "Paid my respects to the families of the men I'd come to know as brothers. We'd put our lives in each other's hands. Five of the six who died had wives and children. One was engaged, came from a large family, nine siblings. I'm the one who had no one back home who'd even miss him. I'm the one who just laid there, while others fought to their death. Me. I made it out alive, thanks to Conrad Mitchell, the only other survivor from our team that day. He pulled me out from under Mark and to safety."

The pain in his eyes broke her heart, but she didn't want to do or say anything that would stop him from getting this burden off his chest.

He pulled his hand away from hers. "Mazy, I'm no one. I stumbled into the job with Jimmy because he knew my mother and reached out to me when I went back home, lost, not fit to be around." With eyes closed, he said, "I was married." He shook his head and looked her squarely in the eyes. "But I wasn't in love. I know that for sure now. I didn't know what love was back then. I never saw it demonstrated. My parents didn't love each other. Hell, my dad left me and my mom without glancing back. I was just a kid. I thought it was my fault. Mom said it was her fault. Truth was, my dad was a selfish prick and if anybody's to blame for the family falling apart it's him."

He brought her hand to his lips and kissed it, then rubbed his cheek against her knuckles. "Being here has opened my eyes to a lot of things. Foremost, the fact is, I need people in my life, people I care about, people who care about me. This crazy little island has embraced me in a way I've never experienced before. Carl, Myrtle, the folks at the restaurant--hell, I've even made friends with Spike, and he was ready to kill me the first day."

In spite of the tears in her eyes, she chuckled, remembering the way Trent hauled ass across the field, Spike pecking at his head.

"People like you, Trent. They really do. I hear them talking about you, joking around about the fire, and the splash you made at Bare Point, what a good sport you've been when they've ribbed you."

A smile warmed his eyes and barely curled the edges of his mouth. "I like the people here. But not you."

She reared back. What the heck was that supposed to mean? Dang. She thought they were having a heart to heart.

He grinned. "Miss Mazelle Washington, I more than like you. Like is not even in the ballpark."

She bit her bottom lip and studied his face, etching this moment into her memory. "I more than like you too." The unsaid word "love" hung in the air between them, winking with a knowing grin.

She cuddled up close to him. He squeezed her tight, kissing the top of her head. In typical male fashion, he ended the conversation abruptly, propped his feet on the coffee table and lifted the remote. He clicked from channel to channel so fast she couldn't tell what was on. Then she saw Jay Leno's watermelon head and Trent said, "No wonder you rarely watch T.V. You need an upgrade, this basic channel crap serves up a whole lot of nothing."

Trent repositioned them both, stretching out on the sofa with his spine to the back of the couch, reclining her so she rested beside him, facing the T.V. He trailed his fingertips up and down her arm, occasionally running his palm across her belly and up and over her breast. Then he traced her nipple through her T-shirt, and her body responded immediately. He tugged the hem of her shirt up, baring her skin and teased her tummy, slipping a couple fingers into the waistband of her sweats.

Yes. Please. Yes. How he'd managed to alter her mood with a few slight strokes she didn't know, but there was no denying he had her revved.

On the T.V., Jay Leno picked up a newspaper and held it up to the camera. "And this one was sent in by Myrtle Pinkerton from Pleasure Island, North Carolina." It was Mazy's shark-crotch picture above the headline that read: *Man's Hand Bitten by Shark. Fifteen Stitches Required.*

Mazy squealed and stiffened.

Trent pulled her closer. His laugh was low and naughty as he pushed his hand into her pants. "I'm not afraid."

Trent awoke to Mazy shaking him. "You gotta get out of here! Come on!"

"What the?" Groggily, he tried to focus on her, but she was a blur of movement, grabbing his clothes off the floor, jerking the covers from is body.

"My dad's coming! You can't be here. I don't know how to explain you." She tugged his hand.

Okay. So she obviously wasn't proud of him, didn't view him as fit to meet her father, but damn. She was freaking the hell out. "You mind telling me what the big deal is here?"

"No time. Please. Please. Come on. He's putting his motorcycle away in the garage. Hurry!"

Crazy as bat shit. That's what she was. She wasn't an underage teen for Christ's sake. He yanked his pants on. She poked him in the back, and stuffed his shirt into his hands. "Damn, woman."

"Go out the back."

She was unbelievable. Why was she so damn panicked about her father being home, or more specifically about her father finding her in bed with a man? She hadn't mentioned that he was insane or anything. She hadn't been a virgin. Surely her father wouldn't be too shocked that his adult daughter was having an adult relationship. Her dad was a biker, not a preacher. What the hell?

She rode his heels down the hall, opened the back door and shoved him onto the deck, then proceeded to toss his shoes at him and slam the door in his face.

She snatched the door back opened, kissed him hard, then ran back in. Slamming the door in his face yet again!

What the fuck?

He had a good mind to march right back in the house and introduce himself to her dad, and show her how ridiculous she was being.

With his hand on the doorknob, he stopped himself. She was being irrational in his eyes, but she obviously viewed things differently. Shit, he didn't know her dad, didn't have the foggiest idea how he'd react if he walked in and found them together. Maybe her old man was like a character from the Sons of Anarchy--a brutal, crazy asshole who'd shoot him dead for screwing his daughter.

Hell, she hadn't said too much about the guy, other than he was cranky most of the time and had abandoned her and Earl right after their mother passed away. What kind of man does that? Coward. Loser. A man just like his own father.

He picked up his shoes and went down the stairs, his shirt slung over his shoulder. This was *not* how he pictured their first morning together going down. He'd made plans to cook her breakfast, serve her in bed, then *serve* her in bed yet again.

Now he was trudging back to the cottage like it was the walk of shame, but he wasn't ashamed of being with Mazy. Nope. She was ashamed of him. Guess he hadn't measure up after all.

CHAPTER FIFTEEN
Daddy's Home

Mazy ran back to her bedroom as soon as she'd thrown Trent out. She felt bad for kicking him out like that, but "Dad, meet Trent McAllister. What brought him to the island? Well, you see, Trent came blazing into town chasing after Earl with the intent to catch and deliver your son to the authorities. What'd Earl do? Nothing, but he's wanted for murder. No, no. Trent decided to be my boyfriend, so he quit looking for Earl. Seriously. He's not looking for clues of Earl's whereabouts at all. Well, he was the first day he got here, of course. He was snooping around in the garage, and I caught him. That's how we met face to face." Yeah, that conversation would go over well.

She threw herself across her bed, her heartbeat thudding loudly in her ears. She hadn't seen her dad in over a year when he'd breezed through with a girl Mazy's age clinging to his back. Why he thought she'd be interested in meeting his flavor of the week was beyond her. Apparently, the girl had insisted on it, saying she wouldn't put out anymore until she'd met the "children." Boy, that had been a real Norman Rockwell painting. Her dad with his white beard and mustache, Albert Einstein hair, brain-fried worse than Ozzy Osbourne's, burping "I love you" across the table at tattoo'd Tina. Tina had purple hair and rock'n'roll deadly mascara smeared halfway down her face. Mazy witnessed this public display of affection in horror, wearing coveralls, grease for rouge, and sporting a chip the size of Alaska on her shoulder.

The front door creaked open. "Mazy! Daddy's home."

Daddy's home? Really? Daddy? Was he in a time warp, forgetting that she'd grown up?

Upon pushing from the bed, she checked herself in the mirror. Jeans, red tank top, hair in a ponytail, no hickies, no signs Trent had been screwing her brains out all night.

Except for that devilish grin caused by the fleeting thought of Trent screwing her brains out all night. They'd gotten busy from one end of the trailer to the other.

Shit. Why'd her dad have to show up now? He'd totally spoiled the whole waking up in Trent's arms moment. She got robbed. Instead of basking in the loving embrace of a hot man, a man who made her feel beautiful and loved, she'd been saddled with the duty of kicking him to the curb like she was some horny housewife who'd gotten caught cheating with the cable guy. Trent deserved better than that. So did she, dammit.

She forced herself into the living room, where her father stood, opening and closing her CD cases, looking for cash. He knew she hid money in some of her favorite albums. Well, she used to do that. The last time he'd cleaned her out, she'd started putting all her funds in the bank like a normal person.

"Hey, Pops. Looking for something?"

He whirled around, gripping a Rachmaninoff piano concerto CD. Busted. Like she'd believe for a minute he was interested in Rachmaninoff. He probably didn't even know how to pronounce the name.

"Hey, darling, just thought I'd listen to me some Ratch man in off. Oh, but lookie here. Hank Williams Jr. Now we're talking." He put the classical CD back and pulled out The Greatest Hits of Little Bocephus.

"You won't find any money over there. Don't waste your time." She glared at him.

"Damn. Nice to see you too."

"What brings you this way, Dad? You down on your luck?"

"No, I'm not down on my luck. Thanks for your touching concern." His sarcasm oozed from every word. "I came to check on you, darling. Got a call from Earl. He was worried about you. Said a bounty hunter was hanging around. Wouldn't tell me much about the charges the law was throwing at him, but those charges won't stick no how. He's got some dirt on the real perpetrators."

"Perpetrators? You been seeing that crazy ass English teacher from Tallahassee again?"

He walked toward her, a twitch in his jaw. The closer he got, the more she could smell him. The man probably hadn't bathed in days. Good God, how could he even stand to be around himself? "You stink! Go take a shower."

"Watch how you talk to me. You keep right on, and I'll take my belt to you. You know I ain't afraid to do it." He snarled.

She rolled her eyes. "I'm twenty-four years old, not eight. You try it, and I'll call Sheriff Meyers. Remember him? Remember the night you spent in the clink after the last time you drew your belt? That was only three years ago. Unless you've gone senile, I suspect you can still recall the event."

His expression softened. "I remember. I remember a lot of things I wish I could forget." He smoothed his wild ass hair and exhaled deeply. "I didn't come here to fight with you, Mazy." He established eye contact with her, unwavering, trapping her with his intense stare. "I love you and Earl. I was worried. I ain't done right by either of ya. I wanted be there when y'all needed me for a change."

Jesus. What was she supposed to do with that?

Trent rode his Harley down Lunar Avenue as the sun sank into the channel where the steamboat, Priscilla, rolled by. Passengers enjoyed their dinner cruise from Wilmington to Crystal Cove and back, an evening ritual he had hoped to experience with Mazy one day. But, he had his doubts that would be happening any time soon. The few text messages he'd received from her since their abrupt goodbye--if you could call it that--had been cryptic at best. He couldn't figure out what was going on. Here it was, after seven, and she hadn't even bothered to call him so they could at least carry on a real conversation.

He was trying his best to refrain from reading into things, interpreting their lack of communication as a sign she wasn't as into him as he thought. She'd been into him last night, and he'd definitely been into her again and again. But a hot night of sex wasn't what they'd shared, not in his book anyway. Sure the sex had been phenomenal. She was far more aggressive and vocal than he'd expected, which he loved, but there was more to it than that--something deeper, more meaningful. It blossomed in the narrow space between them as they'd locked eyes, synchronized breaths, and whispered each other's names in rhythm with their movements, an incantation, sacred. That's exactly what it'd felt like. Sacred.

Then this morning. Errrk, like a needle dragged across a vinyl record.

He pulled into the parking lot of The Sand Dollar Lounge. Parked his bike next to an old orange Pinto with a trash bag taped over the missing passenger window and hung his helmet on his handlebar.

When he stepped inside the darkened pub, country music was blaring on the jukebox, a couple of guys were shooting pool, and a handful of customers were seated at the bar.

An attractive brunette who didn't even look old enough to be in there was mixing drinks, and apparently, running the register as well.

Trent took a seat, waited for her to come over to him.

"What can I get for ya?" She had the most bored expression on her cute face he'd ever seen, like this was the last place she wanted to be.

"Rum and Coke, slice of lime, on the rocks."

"Wanna start a tab or pay by the drink?"

"By the drink." He didn't plan on drinking more than one.

She swiped her long bangs out of her eyes. "Suit yourself. Five dollars."

Her name tag read: Megan. He noticed an opened sketchbook on the counter. If she was the artist who drew the portrait of the drunk at the end of the bar, she was damn good.

She sat his drink in front of him and held out a palm, covering a yawn with her other hand.

He gave her a twenty. "Keep the change."

She flashed him a quizzical look. "You sure?"

"Yes, Megan."

She glanced down at her nametag and then smiled up at him. "Thanks, Trent."

He laughed. Small town. Nowhere to hide. He didn't have the slightest idea how she knew him by name, but he had a feeling Myrtle had something to do with it. Folks kept talking about her blog like it was the local news station.

All eyes in the place traveled to the door when Mazy's father walked in. Trent recognized him from the pictures on Mazy's fridge. It was a bit unnerving how every person in the bar froze at the sight of the man, himself included.

No one spoke to the grizzly biker who looked like he'd rubbed a balloon on his head to get his wiry gray hair to stand straight up. His Rip Van Winkle beard with tobacco stains around his mouth didn't do him any favors either. Of course, any man who'd wear a t-shirt that reads--*If the ol' lady would let me ride her as much as my bike, I'd be home right now*--was obviously not concerned with keeping up appearances.

Mr. Washington walked toward the bar and narrowed his eyes, gave a nod to the old drunk who barely lifted his chin in a gesture of hello. Rafe Washington eyed the young bartender. "Megan Foster. Still pretty as a picture. Where's your dad?"

"Home. Making sure his recliner don't run off." She poured two shots of Southern Comfort in a glass, added a splash of Mountain Dew, and a couple of ice cubes, then slid it over to an empty spot close to Trent.

Rafe sauntered over, took a seat, and reached for the drink. "Good memory. What's your mom up to these days?"

Megan glared at him, didn't answer.

A slow smile slid across Rafe's face. "Oh that's right. I forgot. Sore subject. Sorry 'bout that."

"Sorry is right." Megan mumbled then turned her back to Rafe, busied herself wiping down the counter.

The old man at the end of the bar slid over, positioning himself closer to Mr. Washington, but leaving a couple of empty stools between them. "What brings you to town, Rafe?" His slurred speech was gravelly.

"Nothing much, Bernie. Just checking off my fuck-it list."

The drunk laughed then ended up in a horrible coughing fit.

Rafe faced Trent. "That XR 1200 Harley out there yours?"

Trent nodded, kept his eyes straight ahead.

"Nice ride, man. I got a Street Glide. How many miles you got on yours?"

"Just under 40K." Trent still didn't bother to make eye contact with the man.

"Hell. You ain't even broke it in. What brings ya this way?"

Trent didn't want to tell him the truth. A man like Rafe wasn't the kind to take news about the law after his son very well, which is probably why Mazy panicked this morning. Didn't take much to figure it out. Trent faced the guy. "Just passing through. Heard there was an ostrich farm on the island, thought I'd check it out."

"The ostriches. Yeah. They've been drawing in tourists for years. Have you seen 'em race? Wait, I think that's in September. Megan? When is that big ostrich league race?"

"Labor Day weekend."

"That's right. Wing Fling, the big end of summer festival. Well, you should come on back Labor Day weekend. It's a blast to watch. What's your name, Bo? I'm Rafe."

"Trent. I'll keep the race in mind. Sounds entertaining."

"It's a hoot. My daughter Mazy loves it. She even jockeyed one year, but when they found out she was underage, they disqualified her. Then the ostrich she'd trained on died and broke her heart. She ain't ridden since. At least I don't think she has. I could be wrong. Not like I've kept up with her very well." Sadness shown in the man's brown eyes.

"Families lose touch with one another. It happens."

"Losing touch. That's one way of putting it. Sorry ass dads run off and forget their kids is another way. Shit. I got my work cut out for me."

Megan leaned across the bar, eyed Rafe. "Is that why you're here? To patch things up between you and Mazy?"

"Worth a try."

Megan smiled. "That drink's on me. Want another?"

Rafe smiled. "Thank you. Believe I will."

Ted walked in, his gaze went from Rafe to Trent and back to Rafe. Then he leveled Trent with a scowl.

Megan's eyes rounded then she stared at Trent, shook her head slightly.

He wasn't sure what all these strange looks were supposed to mean, but he sensed both of them were trying to send him some kind of warning. He chugged down the last of his drink. "Well, nice meeting y'all."

Rafe nodded. "Take it easy, man."

"You too." Trent patted the bar. "Megan, thanks for the drink. Y'all have a good evening."

"Take care." She reached for a bottle on the top shelf.

As Trent walked past Ted, Ted met his gaze and said, "Watch yourself."

Trent didn't react. Was that a warning, or a threat?

Didn't matter. He could handle Ted or Rafe, whatever that "watch yourself" was supposed to mean. Ted needed to be the one watching himself. He was lucky Trent was taking the high road.

As he exited the bar, the evening sky was a dusky gray, lights across the channel were reflected on the water. Mazy wasn't being held up by her dad right now. So, why hadn't she called?

Mazy sat on the cottage porch with Myrtle, awaiting Trent's return.

"You'll work things out with your dad. I know he's a gruff SOB, but he's got a good side too. We all got an ass end, you know? His is just bigger than most."

Mazy couldn't help but laugh as she wiped her eyes with the sleeve of her hoodie. "I've just never heard him apologize before, not even to my mom. I want to forgive him. I do, but--"

Myrtle rocked a little faster. "You have to forgive him a little piece at a time. That's the secret. Everything all at once is too much for anybody to let go of. No, just think of one thing that's been haunting you. One small thing--not the big stuff now--I'm talking maybe the fact he ain't ever so much as called you on your birthday. Start there. Then tomorrow, pick something else."

"How am I gonna tell him about Trent?"

Myrtle twisted her mouth. "Let's not tackle that one right off. Meet me at the restaurant for breakfast at seven tomorrow, and I'll tell the girls to join us so we can put our heads together about that."

"Okay." Mazy's pulse accelerated when she caught sight of Trent coming across the field on his Harley.

Myrtle stood. "All right. Here he comes. Remember what I told ya. Just tell him how you feel about him and some of the stunts your dad has pulled in the past. It'll be okay."

"Thank you." Mazy couldn't take her eyes off Trent. When Myrtle's golf cart started moving, Mazy flinched. Myrtle waved and headed back to Carl's place.

Trent rode up to the porch. Propped his bike on the kickstand and took off his helmet. He sat there for a few minutes, staring at her, making her nervous as hell.

CHAPTER SIXTEEN
Union

Mazy couldn't tell if Trent was angry or hurt, maybe both. He walked up the stairs and over to her, held out his hand and pulled her out of the rocker. As he led her inside the cottage, he squeezed her hand and offered her a weak smile.

Once they settled onto the couch facing each other, she said, "I'm really sorry about kicking you out this morning. I panicked. I'm sure that must have seemed ridiculous to you."

"I was a bit stunned. I won't lie." He gathered her hands in his.

She cleared her throat, trying to think of exactly how to explain herself. "My dad...he's...well he's a real hot head. I didn't know how to introduce y'all, what to say about how you and I met."

"I gathered as much. You figure it out yet?"

She wasn't sure how to read Trent. He was acting a little too calm and controlled for her comfort. It was like he was being very careful what he said, as if anything he said could be used against him in a court of law.

He lifted an eyebrow, awaiting her response.

"I...I haven't quite figured it out. I wish I could say otherwise. Any suggestions?"

"I met your dad at The Sand Dollar Lounge."

She gasped. Oh shit.

Trent laced his fingers with hers. "I didn't tell him I knew you or Earl. We didn't talk about what I did for a living before coming to the island. Don't worry."

Thank God. "What did y'all talk about?"

"Not much. We only hung out for a few minutes, but in that short time, he mentioned you. Talked about wanting to make amends."

Her father had said that? To other people? What had gotten into him? Did he have a terminal illness? It was shocking when he'd told her himself, but to say it in public, that was way out of character for him.

"Mazy, I think you and your dad just need some time together without bringing me into the picture, at least for a day or two. I'm not going anywhere. Unless you want me to, in which case, I'll leave."

"Don't you dare leave me!" She blurted that out without thinking. She tugged a hand free and covered her mouth with it.

He gently moved her hand away. "Like I said, I'm not going anywhere."

"Everything's so complicated now."

"Life is complicated, Mazy. But, your father is putting forth an effort to be a part of your life. I know how badly he's hurt you in the past by not being around when you needed him most. You owe it to yourself and to him to try and work out your differences. My dad left when I was kid, and that was that. If he came walking through the door right now, and said he was sorry and wanted to be a part of my life, I'm not sure how I'd react, but I know I'd be a ball of emotions, confused for sure. But the bottom line is, a relationship with my father is something I've longed for, even while pissed at him. People never outgrow the desire to have their parents tell them that they love them and want to be in their lives. Take some time. Focus on finding your footing with your dad and making things better between the two of you so you can both move forward."

Her shoulders deflated back down to their normal position. She hadn't even known she'd been so tense, until she felt herself relax.

Trent opened his arms. She moved closer and put her head on his chest. As he wrapped his arms around her, she closed her eyes, breathing him in.

He nudged her chin up and looked into her eyes. "We okay?"

"Better than okay." As the words left her mouth he dipped his head and kissed her softly, then again, and again.

She reached up and ran her fingers in his hair, drew him closer, deepening the kiss. A dizzy, yet safe, sensation filled her. There was no heated sexual energy coursing through her —not like it had last night when they'd kissed on the couch at her place. This was different, more comforting, like she and Trent weren't just hooking up, but building a strong foundation for a lasting relationship. Nothing about it felt suffocating. She had no urge to run in the other direction like she had when her previous boyfriend suggested they move in together. This time she was falling without fear, because Trent was there to catch her.

Trent wanted to be the man Mazy could count on, let her know what they shared wasn't a fling, but far more than that, at least for him.

He pulled her onto his lap. She straddled him, his hands on her bottom. "Mazy, whatever you want from me, it's yours. However much, or however little, It's up to you."

She stared down at him and whispered, "Make love to me."

He stood with her legs wrapped around him and carried her to bed.

Once he'd placed Mazy in the center of the mattress, he turned on a CD player by the bed, curious to see her reaction to the percussion ensemble compilation he'd purchased in her honor.

"Marimba?" She reclined on her elbows, tilted her head, and listened a bit more. When the auxiliary percussion joined in the mix, she fell back on the bed. "I can't believe you! This is awesome."

He smiled. "You like?"

"Yes!" Her eyes widened as the timpani added a low sounding riff. Then the music grew quiet, the delicate wind chimes holding the focus.

He undressed and stood at the foot of the bed, moving his body to the sound of the slow drums. He rolled a condom onto his erection, letting her see that he was ready whenever she was. Each accented pop on a snare drum elicited a pelvic thrust from him.

Mazy giggled, fluffed a pillow and sat up, with her back to the headboard, enjoying the show.

He kept his face serious, even though a part of him wanted to laugh.

After a few minutes of silliness, passion flickered in her eyes, and she began to touch her breasts through her thin tank top.

"Show me." He pinched his own nipples to demonstrate.

She shimmied out of her shirt and mimicked his movements.

"That's it, baby. Lose the pants." He stroked himself to the deep melodic tune carried by the contrabass marimba.

Mazy moaned. "Holy shit, you're so sexy. I love this."

"Lose the pants." He repeated and placed a knee on the bed, then grabbed the hem of one of her pantlegs. She unzipped her jeans, lifted her hips and slid them down. He jerked them off of her and let them fly across the room. "Pull those panties to the side and show me."

She did, spreading herself with her fingers. She was glistening for him.

"Pat your clit to this beat." He pointed to the CD player right at the moment the tambourine played a syncopated rhythm that repeated.

She closed her eyes, her head fell back, and she tapped and rubbed herself for him, until she was crying out.

"Don't stop." He wanted her to come before he'd even

touched her.

She whimpered and grinded her hips into the air. God, she blew his mind.

Barely opening her eyes, she looked up at him. "I want you."

"Don't stop." He ripped her panties off of her, leaving her spread naked before him. "Listen to the music, follow the rhythm." He knew the drumming would increase speed at any moment and when it did, she'd come hard.

She panted and tensed. "I can't hold it in."

"I don't want you to." The music quickened. She rubbed faster and came for him, her body twitching, and thrashing.

When she slowly grew calm again, with her legs together, He opened her thighs wide and lowered his head to lick her to the currently calm music.

Bathing her plush folds with his tongue, he watched her response, not wanting to miss a single flash of pleasure on her face.

When her head began to toss side to side, lost in the music and the sensation of his tongue, he flipped her onto her knees, placed her hands on the rungs of the brass bed frame and slid his head under her ripe mound. Directing her hips with his hands, he forced her to grind until she found the groove again.

"Mmmm." He moaned into her sex, loving the way she was moving over him, taking pleasure from his tongue.

He stroked himself, just enough to soothe the ache, without pushing him to the edge.

The bed shook as she rocked, tugging at the headboard. "Trent. I'm going to come again."

That's what he wanted to hear. He grabbed her hips and made her keep taking it, until she trembled above him.

"Stop, stop, stop, stop. Oh God. I can't take anymore. Ooo." She sat back on his chest and smiled down at him.

The music tirelessly continuing, just as he intended to do.

He loved the sensation of her wetness over his heart.

Looking down into his eyes, she caressed his hair, his face, traced a finger over his lips, then slid down his body and kissed him.

He grabbed her face in his hands, caught her gaze in his. "I'm in love with you, Mazy."

She gasped.

He watched her thoughts take shape behind her eyes, as the emotions played on her face--shock, tenderness, elation. Then tears welled in her eyes and a smile trembled on her lips.

He smiled. "I love you."

She brought her mouth to his and whispered, "I love you too."

And as their lips met, he pushed himself up inside her.

She shuddered. "I love you." Again she professed her heart against his hungry mouth, and he returned her love.

In the heated exchange of verbalizing what their hearts felt, they found their own rhythm that expressed the beauty of the moment.

His lovely drummer girl unleashed everything inside of her, and it washed over him, sending him skyrocketing into delirium.

Breathless, their sweat-slicked bodies entwined, she trembled in the afterglow of their lovemaking. She whispered, "God, baby. I feel transported into some state of being I didn't even know existed. I can't explain it."

He felt it too. "That's because true love is beyond language. You don't need to explain it to me. You took me there with you. It's not something you can experience alone."

She gazed into his eyes. "No. No one can go there alone. I'm so glad we have each other."

He pulled her against him to rest her head upon his chest.

As he stroked her hair, he whispered. "I'm the happiest I've ever been, because of you."

"Me too." Her quiet voice tickled across his chest as the music faded and the final resonating shimmers from a suspended cymbal dissipated into the air. "Me too."

When Mazy entered Reel to Real Good, Myrtle, Louise, Sam, Kendal, and Leah were seated at a large round table for their breakfast meeting. Mazy eyed the quiche, pastries, fruit salad, juice, coffee--the works. Wow. She loved a big breakfast. Mazy sat in the empty seat between Myrtle and Kendal and greeted everyone good morning.

Myrtle didn't waste any time getting down to business. "Glad everybody could make it. We all know what a knot head Rafe can be, so I figured the more people around when he meets Trent, the better. He's less likely to cause a scene. Plus, we can show him that Trent's a good guy."

Kendal said, "I'm sorry. I thought we were here to help Mazy figure out a way to patch things up with her dad. I didn't know this had anything to do with Trent. What's going on?"

All the women looked at Mazy. "Trent and I, well, we're in love. I know it's sudden, and y'all probably think I'm nuts, but I love him so much. And he loves me."

Myrtle chimed in. "Well, I didn't know things had gotten to the love stage, but that's all the more reason to make sure the meeting between Rafe and Trent goes well."

Kendal shook her head like she couldn't process this. "Wait. When did this happen? Last I heard you were flirting with Ted, and that was just a few nights ago. How can you be in love with Trent?"

Leah spoke up. "Kendal, Mazy was just trying to make Trent jealous cause she thought he and I had gone on a date.

She's not interested in Ted. Never has been. You know that."

Sam wiped her mouth with a napkin. "Listen, I've liked Trent from day one, and I'm probably the hardest one in the crowd to charm. Sometimes love comes on quickly. At first, I couldn't imagine you and Trent together romantically. But watching y'all interact, I see the spark between you two. Personally, Mazy, I think you and Trent make a cute couple. Brock said Trent quit his job right after he got here. So, there's really no reason why anyone should have a problem with the two of you getting together, including your father."

Kendal stared at Sam. Leah patted Kendal's leg. "This works out for you. Now, Ted will stop chasing Mazy."

"So. What do I care?" Kendal gulped juice, her big hazel eyes scanning the table, her face turning redder by the second.

Louise slurped her coffee, then said. "Relax, Kendal, we all know you got a thing for Ted. I don't blame you. He's my favorite piece of man candy on the island. You got good taste. Unfortunately for me, I'm too old for him. But you. You're young and gorgeous. Don't be embarrassed for having a crush on that man. In fact, I have a few naughty craft projects I've made of him in my private collection--a sock with his face on it that fits on the horn of my ostrich saddle, a collage of him in various states of dress. And my favorite is a body pillow that goes between your legs to keep your hips aligned. That one's brought on some sweet dreams many nights. MmmMmmMmm. I'll make one for you too."

"Geeze, Louise!" Kendal covered face. "This conversation isn't happening."

Myrtle giggled. "My oh my, Louise, you've been holding out on me. But I like the way you think. You're giving me some ideas of my own. We might need to schedule another craft making day real soon."

Leah smiled and said, "I just love you two ladies. I hope I'm as much fun when I'm your age."

Myrtle widened her eyes. "You're sweet, sugar, but if I was your age, with your looks, and single...Ooooweee...I'd be one happy ho."

Louise raised her water glass. "I'll drink to that." She grinned at Myrtle. "Just one day in Leah's body and my Miss Puss would be sending me a thank you note."

Everyone at the table busted out laughing, except for Kendal, she still had her face in her hands, elbows on the table. "This conversation is *not* happening."

Sam ate the last bite of her muffin and pushed her plate forward. "Okay, let's get serious here. I remember how petrified I was to meet Brock's folks, and he and I were already married. I was so worried they wouldn't like me, and there was no reason for my fears, but Trent, dang, I can only imagine how he must feel. Lucky for me, Brock's family welcomed me with opened arms, made me really feel like a part of their family. Carl told Brock that Trent doesn't have a family to speak of. We really need to make this work, for Trent's sake, as well as Mazy's. And no offense, Mazy, but your dad can be a real shit. This ain't gonna be easy."

Myrtle sat up straight. "I think I got it figured out, though. So, as I was saying...I took down all my blog posts about Trent and put the word out for everyone to be hush hush around Rafe. Now, what I was thinking is, we could have a party. Get a bunch of people from the island together, including some of Rafe's old buddies, even though I'm not overly fond of some of them, I'm willing to set that aside. Hell, I'll call it a welcome home party for Rafe. Then he'll have to come. He wouldn't dare miss his own party, a chance to be the center of attention. We'll stage people here and there to talk about what a great guy Trent is, how they are so glad he quit his job and plans to stay on the island.

Then, I'll slide in there with information about what Trent's job was, and Carl and I can make sure he knows Trent isn't after Earl."

Louise said, "Then I'll come up and mention he and Mazy look cute together, point them out in the crowd."

"Yeah, that'll work." Myrtle nodded to Louise.

Sam said, Brock and I can walk over with Trent and Mazy to meet Rafe, that way if Rafe flares up, Brock can handle it."

Leah grinned. "This is going to work. I'll cover the food."

Kendal twisted her mouth.

Leah patted Kendal's hand. "What's wrong?"

Kendal released a big breath. "I want to help."

Mazy reached over and squeezed Kendal's hand. "Just having you there for moral support is a help."

Kendal smiled. "I'll be the DJ. That's what I'll do. I'll keep your dad's favorite songs playing. I know what he likes."

Mazy smiled. "That will be perfect. He'll have no choice but to be in a good mood then."

Myrtle patted the table. "Ladies, I think we got ourselves a plan. I'll start getting things lined up today, and we'll finalize everything during set breaks tonight."

Louise stood, winced as she straightened her back. "I'll bring you that body pillow, Kendal."

Kendal's head snapped up, her eyes as big as a lemur's. "I'm good. No...no....thank you."

"Okay, suit yourself, I'll bring the saddle sock instead."

CHAPTER SEVENTEEN
Creek

Mazy stepped inside her front door to find her father sitting at the kitchen table. She was hoping he'd still be passed out on the couch, like he was when she left this morning.

He pushed to his feet. "Look what the cat dragged in. You stayed out all night. Did he kick you out, or did you sneak out of his bed this morning like a little slut?"

His hateful words were like a slap in the face. Why was he being this way? Hadn't he come home to make amends?

She tensed and stiffened her backbone. There was only one way to deal with him when he got like this. She was going to have to stand up to him. Be as nasty to him as he was to her. Otherwise, he'd sniff out her fear, her wounded feelings, and crush her.

She put her hand on her hip and glared at him. "Who are you talking about? The only sluts I know are the ones you bring home like they're some sort of skank trophy."

"Does the name Trent McAllister mean anything to you?" The creases in his brow resembled weathered wood as he stalked toward her, hatred pouring off him.

How'd he find out about Trent? Did someone engage him in a tell-all at the bar? She assumed he went to the bar, judging from the way he reeked of beer when she walked by him this morning. Oh no. What if he turned violent?

Stand your ground, Mazy.

Toe to toe, she stared up at him. "Yes. The name means a great deal to me."

"A great deal? Girl, you're a piece of work, you know that? Ted and some of the boys told me all about Mr. Trent McAllister. You been spreading your legs for the cock who's trying to fuck your brother."

She trembled beneath his bitter snarl, but tried not to let him know his words had any impact on her. "You're the one who fucked Earl. You fucked us both up the day you turned your back on us. The flowers on Mama's grave were still fresh. You didn't even attempt to settle the bill at the funeral home. You just split. Earl wouldn't have ever gotten in any trouble if he wasn't trying to find a way to pay the bills that were your responsibility."

Rafe drew his hand up like he was about to slap her into next week.

She trembled inside. His blows always hurt her heart as much as her body. There was a time she would have cowered, if he'd so much as lunged at her. Not anymore. She knew how he worked.

She lifted her chin. "Go on then! Do it! Prove how mean you are, but don't act like you give a shit about me or Earl. The only person you care about is yourself."

He lowered his hand and balled it into a fist. "I ought to break your jaw for that."

"And I ought to kick you to the curb and never let you step foot on my land again. That's right. My land. Not yours. Mama knew what she was doing, taking you off the deed."

"You're one stupid bitch." He turned his back to her.

She released a deep breath and wiped her sweaty palms on her jeans. So much for the big welcome home party plans. Shit. This little fatherly visit wasn't going to end well. No chance Trent would be welcomed into the family now.

Rafe paced the living room, hands in his pocket. Then he faced her, pointed his finger at her nose. "You can think what you want about me, but tell me this, how would your sainted mother feel about you running around with that bounty hunter, huh? You think she'd be proud of you for hooking up with the man two steps away from throwing Earl to the wolves? Think on that. If you're stupid enough to believe that man has any interest in you beyond what you can tell him about your brother, you're probably stupid enough to believe *anything* he tells you. I heard he's been saying he ain't on the case anymore. Yeah. Right."

"And you think you got it all figured out. You haven't been around for a year, and overnight, you magically know everything. You say you're here to make amends, do right by me and Earl. Huh. Nice way of showing it. Thanks, *Daddy*."

"All right." He sucked his teeth. "I didn't want to have to do this." He pulled out his phone and thumbed in a number. "Let's see how Earl feels about all this."

"No!" She reached for his phone. Her father held it up in the air, put the call on speaker. It rang.

Earl answered. "Hello? Dad?"

She tried to climb her father to rip the phone from his grasp.

Rafe pushed her away. "Yep. It's me. I got some bad news. Mazy's been sleeping with the bounty hunter, Trent McAllister. Here, I'll let her tell you about it." He sneered and handed her the cell.

She mouthed, "I hate you," at her father. She clicked off of speaker and held the phone to her ear. "Earl?"

"Mazy, what's he talking about?"

"Earl, listen, Trent's not a bounty hunter anymore."

"Shit. The old man wasn't joking around? You *are* fucking the bounty hunter?"

"Hear me out. It's not what you think."

"Mazy. I never dreamed you'd turn on me." His voice trembled. "I ain't got time for this. Gotta go." He hung up on her.

She burst into tears, threw her father's android at him. It bounced off his chest and landed by her drums. She screamed at her dad. "You need to get the hell out of here. Now!"

He walked over to her drums and bent to pick up his phone.

Her own cell chirped and she reached into her pocket.

Her dad was on her in a split second, pinned her arms to her side, pried the device out of her hand, and stared at the screen. "Just what I thought. Loverboy." He dragged her to the backdoor, opened it, and tossed her cell into the creek. "Now, you think long and hard before you talk to that son of bitch again."

He let her go.

She shoved him away. "Asshole. Get the hell out!"

"Gladly." He walked out the door and down the steps without glancing back.

She wiped her eyes and rushed toward the creek, looking for the sparkly purple device, but it was nowhere to be seen.

She collapsed onto the boulder by the waterfall. As much as she hated her dad right then, she couldn't help but feel sad that he may never return. That wasn't how her mother would have wanted things to go. And what about Earl? God. Would he ever speak to her again? Maybe she should have stayed away from Trent from the beginning like she'd planned. She lowered her head to her hands and sobbed so hard she felt as if she'd been turned inside out.

Trent paced the living room. That damn sinking feeling in his stomach wouldn't let up. Mazy hadn't returned any of his text messages. She hadn't called him. He'd told her he'd give her some space, but something was wrong. He just knew it.

He walked across the field and down the dirt path. As he crossed the street, he spotted a gold Lexus with tinted windows parked in Mazy's yard. He crept through the woods. When he neared the Lexus, he noted its South Carolina personalized license plate: ZeeMan. Oh shit. Vic's top competitor.

Two men in suits were talking in the garage. He inched

his way over to the door, crouched behind a bush by the entrance and listened.

A tall guy with a bald head looked down at a short man with blond hair. The tall one said, "I wish Zee would lay off the girl. She was telling us the truth about her old man throwing her phone in the creek. We fished it out. It's useless. Why is Zee still torturing her? She doesn't know anything. You can see it in her eyes. She ain't lying."

Jesus. Zee had Mazy. Trent's blood boiled. The thought of calling 911 crossed his mind, then he squelched the notion. Country bumpkin police could screw this up so fast. He was better off taking care of business alone. He switched his phone to camcorder, pressed record and held it out, just enough to capture the guys in the garage on camera. But even if he didn't get their faces all that clearly, he'd get their voices for sure. He might need some hard evidence later.

He forced himself to remain calm instead of barreling into the garage. If he were detected, things could get out of hand in an instant. He wasn't going to take any chances with Mazy's life at stake.

The blond man said, "You're a real idiot, man. He ain't letting that girl live. You think she'd keep her mouth shut about us? Get real."

Kill her? Only one dying today was going to be one of them. Maybe all of them. He zoomed in on every detail, as he mentally went into combat mode.

The tall one responded, "Nobody said anything to me about killing her. I didn't sign up for that shit."

"Let me clue you in on a few details then. You walk, you're a dead man. Consider yourself signed up. Zee's gonna get as much information as he can outa the bitch, then he's gonna slide her cute little body under this car. When he releases the lift, the jeep will crush her like a bug. We'll make sure it looks like an accident, and we're gone. When Earl gets wind of her death, he'll come out of hiding. Then it'll just be the matter of staging his suicide. Guy loses a sister, can't come to terms with it, scared to go to her funeral, worried he'll be found. Knowing if he's found, he's going to jail. Depressing enough to make anyone want to kill themselves."

Thank you very much for all the information, assholes. You're digging your own grave.

The tall man nodded, finally catching on. "And with the number one suspect gone, the one with all the evidence pointing at him, nobody is going to come looking for Zee."

"Now you're getting it." The short man patted the other guy's back.

"I don't know, man. I wish you would've told me this earlier. Taking two lives when the law ain't even looking for Zee?"

"Like I said. You know too much to be allowed to just walk away, bro. Deal with it."

Deal with it is right. Trent was ready to give them both a concussion to deal with. Peeking into the garage, Trent spotted a roll of duct tape and a tire iron near the door. When both men had their backs turned, he slid his phone in the pocket of the crappy golf shirt he'd found in the closet. The camera lens portion of the phone just peeked out over the top of the pocket. Excellent. He kept the camera rolling. He reached around and grabbed the tape and tire iron, then ducked back out of sight.

One of the men walked toward the garage door. "I'm going to check on Zee. See if he needs any help."

When the bald man stepped out of the garage and walked toward the trailer, Trent crept up behind him and whacked him on the back of the skull. The guy fell like a sack of potatoes, knocked out cold. He taped the unconscious man's mouth shut, bound his wrists together behind his back, then taped his ankles together. He dragged the guy behind a nearby bush and crept back to the garage. One down, two to go.

Trent slipped back around to the opened garage door and peered in. The squat blonde guy toyed with the car lift, watching the tireless jeep go up and down. Trent sneaked up behind the guy and clubbed him with the tire iron, back of the skull, just like his friend. Out in one swing. He taped this one the same way and dragged him off into the woods behind the garage.

Rooster squealed and stuck his nose to the wire fence around his pen. Trent eased over to the pig and unlatched the gate. Rooster trotted over to him and sat at his feet. "I need your help, little buddy." The pig blinked up at him, attentive.

Trent scooped him up, placed a hand over his snout, and whispered, "No racket 'til I give you the signal." The pig grunted, his sounds muffled by Trent's hand.

Once on the back deck, Trent eased the backdoor open, turned Rooster loose inside the trailer, and nudged him down the hall.

The pig bounded toward the kitchen, sounding his crowing alarm for all he was worth.

Zee screamed like a five year old in a haunted house. Trent caught a glimpse of Mazy tied to a chair. Her head was slumped forward, blood in her hair and on her clothes. He couldn't see her face. Was she dead? Was he too late? She tugged against her restraints. Thank God.

Zee was completely distracted by Rooster, just as Trent planned.

As soon as Zee, who looked like Hulk Hogan, turned his back, gawking at Rooster, Trent walloped the man hard. Zee fell to his knees, then toppled face forward. Trent's pot-bellied sidekick barely had a chance to scoot away without getting crushed beneath the weight of the Neanderthal doing a face-plant on the linoleum.

Trent wanted to check on Mazy, but knew better than to turn his back on an unsecured enemy. He taped Zee like the others then lunged to Mazy.

He brushed her hair from her face. God. That maniac. "Mazy?" Jesus! Her face! That bastard had used her beautiful face for a punching bag.

Her mouth moved, but she didn't say anything, at least nothing he could hear.

He thumbed 911 into his phone. Then, in a blind rage, he continuously kicked the shit out of Zee while the man was still unconscious.

"Trent. Stop." Mazy's weak voice caused him to freeze. His body trembled. He dropped the tire iron, fell to his knees, and crawled over to her.

"Mazy. Hang on, baby." He gently cradled her battered face in his hands. Her eyes cracked open, tiny puffy slits.

She gurgled and bloody drool oozed from her swollen mouth. He thought he saw her trying to smile. She mumbled, "My hero."

Tears filled his eyes.

Then ever so faintly, she whispered. "Rooster, the warrior pig."

CHAPTER EIGHTEEN
Bows

A group of voices woke Mazy. She could barely open her eyes. Her nose itched. She reached up to scratch. Something was in her nostrils. Tubes. Oxygen tubes?

An IV was stuck in the back of her hand. The hospital. She must be in the hospital.

Her jaw ached, and she couldn't open or close her mouth.

She tried to focus on the faces encircling her.

Myrtle's distinct voice caught her attention. "She's waking up, y'all. Mazy? Mazy, honey? Can you hear me?"

Carl grumbled. "Of course she can hear you. The doctor didn't say nothing about her ears being hurt."

"Hush up, or I'm going box your ears, you old grouch." Myrtle leaned in close enough for Mazy to make out her fuzzy blue hair. "He didn't mean nothing by that. He ain't slept a wink all night. Refused to leave your side, the old coot. You had us all worried sick. Let me get the nurse in here." Myrtle pushed the call button.

She'd been in the hospital all night? Why couldn't she remember anything?

A nurse said, "May I help you?"

Myrtle hollered. "She's waking up. Come give her some pain medicine, would ya?"

Mazy waved, trying to indicate she didn't need any more drugs. She was having a hard enough time focusing as it was. And even though her face was throbbing, she wasn't in any excruciating pain. Mostly, she felt like she'd just gotten off the teacup ride at Disney.

Memories of a big man beating her and threatening her drifted to mind, then the image of Rooster in a red superhero cape popped into her head. What the hell?

Trent's face moved in her line of vision beside Myrtle's. He was so handsome. God she loved him.

He smiled. "You feeling woozy?"

"Yeah." Jesus. She sounded like a bullfrog.

She heard laughter and looked around.

Leah, Sam, Brock, Kendal, and Louise they were all there too. She lifted her hand and wiggled her fingers. "Hey."

Leah grabbed her foot and squeezed. "Hey, Mazy. Let me know if you're hungry. Jack made your favorite lobster bisque. The nurse said she'd heat it up whenever you feel like eating. I figured the soup would be easy for you since you won't have to chew it."

Kendal placed a stuffed pig beside Mazy. "They wouldn't let me bring Rooster in. This is the closest I could get."

Sam and Brock stepped up to the opposite side of the bed from Trent and Myrtle. Sam said, "We're babysitting Rooster for ya. He and Princess are getting along great. They were cuddled up in Princess's bed this morning. I took some pictures. They're on the windowsill with all the flowers from people all over the island. Spencer outdid herself. The arrangements are gorgeous. The stargazer lilies are from me and Brock."

How sweet. But damn. Information overload. Why was everyone acting like she'd be here for a while longer? What had happened to her? She didn't notice any bandages or casts on her body, but she felt plenty of bandages on her face and head.

Carl wedged himself in between Myrtle and Trent. "I got up with your dad. He's with Earl. Everybody's okay. Trent turned those fellas over to the police. I suspect an officer will be paying you a visit later on to ask some questions so they can finish their report."

Earl? Her dad? Oh God. She remembered now. Her heart squeezed at the memory of the argument with her father and the conversation with Earl.

Louise stood behind Myrtle and peered over the top of

her head. "I made a giant get well card for you. Everybody on the island signed it. I even got Robirrrda and Rooster's paw print. Footprint? Hoofprint? Aww, hell. You know what I mean."

Mazy looked up at Trent, wanting to know more information. She vaguely recalled him beating up the guy who'd hit her.

She wanted to speak to Trent, ask some questions, thank him for saving her life, again. But she couldn't talk beyond one syllable words like *hey* and *yeah*.

He seemed to read her mind. He nodded. "I'll get the doctor to come in here and explain what all he did, but basically, your jaw's been wired shut so the bone can fuse back together. You've had some stitches on your face, but the scarring will be minimal he said. You're fine otherwise. They were able to reduce the swelling in your brain quickly enough that you sustained no permanent damage. That was a relief. You're going to be all right. Oh, and by the way, I lied and claimed to be your husband to get around the privacy act nonsense so the doctor would tell me what was going on with you. I'm surprised he fell for the lie so easily. If he calls you Mrs. McAllister, don't act surprised."

Myrtle giggled. "That's a crappy proposal. He'll do a better job of it later. Won't you, Trent?"

Trent frowned at Myrtle. "I wasn't proposing. Not that I won't, but that wasn't it."

Everyone started laughing. His face turned bright red. He looked around the room. "Jesus. You people. Do you embarrass everybody like this?"

Myrtle grinned up at Trent. "Consider it your initiation. Now you're one of us."

Brock said, "Bollocks. You got off bloody easy, mate. You don't even want to know how they initiated me into the club."

Mazy wanted to laugh right along with her friends, but could only cough a ha ha.

The next morning…

Mazy woke up to the sound of Earl's voice. "Mazy, me and Dad are here. Can you hear me?" He gently stroked her arm.

She opened her eyes to find him bent over her, his face red, chin trembling. She put her hand over his and whispered, "Yeah."

Her dad's face came into view. He took one look at her and broke down in tears, knelt by her bed and put is head on her stomach. "I'm such a fool. I'm sorry, babygirl. I shouldn't have left. If I had stayed…" His sobs took his breath and he couldn't finish his sentence.

She stroked her father's messy hair. He was clean and dressed in a nice shirt and pair of slacks. He'd even trimmed his beard and mustache. Why was he cleaned up? He didn't need to get dressed up to come the hospital.

Earl threw himself over her and her father and hugged them, crying. "It's my fault. I should know better than to hang out with criminals. It's my fault. I'm so sorry."

The comforting weight of her brother and her father and their heartfelt apologies caused all her own sorrow to bubble to the surface, and she balled her eyes out with them. They all had so much pent up emotions to release. It was a deluge of tears. None of them were able to speak, but somehow everything that needed to be said was communicated through their tears, their exchanged glances, and their loving embrace.

Trent entered the hospital room with a fresh cup of coffee and a new crossword puzzle book.

Earl and her dad pulled away and snatched some tissue

from the box by her bed. They dabbed their eyes and blew their nose, trying to pull themselves together. Earl placed the box of tissues at her side. She helped herself and dried her eyes.

Rafe approached Trent. "Hi Trent. I believe we met the other day. I want to thank you..." Her father started crying again, stomped his foot, and faced the window.

Earl came up beside her dad and put his hand on his father's trembling shoulder. "My dad wants to thank you for saving Mazy's life. And so do I." He stepped away from their dad and held his hand out to Trent. "I'm Earl."

Trent moved his coffee to his left hand and shook Earl's hand. "Nice to finally meet you properly. Mazy thinks the world of you."

Earl swallowed hard and nodded, still shaking Trent's hand. "I think the world of..." His words trailed off and he moved closer to Trent and hugged him. "Jesus, man. We'd both be dead if it wasn't for you."

Trent held his coffee away from him, with the crossword book under his arms, his eyes revealing shock and awkwardness as he looked over Earl's shoulder at Mazy.

Her heart overflowed, and she smiled a ridiculously painful smile, but her mouth simply couldn't be controlled.

Her father rushed over to the men. Took Trent's coffee and book and sat it on the chair by the door, then embraced Trent and Earl.

This wasn't the welcome home party she and the girls had planned, but it certainly felt like a welcome home made in heaven. She lifted the picture of her mother from the table still positioned over her lap from breakfast. She gazed at the sunset, her mother's billowing white dress, her flaming red hair on the wind and silently said, "Thank you, Mama."

All three men pulled themselves back together and gathered around her.

Earl said, "Dad and I just came from the police station. All charges against me have been dropped. Thanks to the quick thinking of Trent, the plans these guys had to kill you and me both were caught on video. One of the guys got roped into more than he bargained for, and he sang like a canary, confessed everything. That video and confession, plus some of the evidence I was able to scrounge up on my own made it pretty cut and dried. My name is in the clear, and it's gonna stay that way. I'm only associating myself with people on the up and up like Trent from now on."

Trent clapped Earl on the back. Earl smiled over his shoulder at Trent.

Rafe took a few deep breaths in and out. "I know one thing. I ain't going no where. I nearly lost you two kids before we had a chance to become a family again. From now on, my butt's staying right here on the island." He looked at Trent. "I hope you're staying too."

Trent nodded. "I am."

"Glad to hear it. I'll never be able to thank you enough for all you've done for my kids, but I hope we can be friends."

Trent nodded. "I'd like that. I'd like that a lot."

A few months later...

Mazy looked around her brand new kitchen, admiring the granite countertops and shiny new stainless steel appliances. Her dad, Earl, and Trent had all pitched in to move the construction process along. She and Trent had barely finished decorating and arranging all their new furniture. The house looked like it should be in Southern Living magazine. She could hardly believe it was hers.

She cut Trent, her father, and Earl each a slice of pecan pie after their Thanksgiving dinner.

Earl scraped the remaining food from the dinner plates and ran the garbage disposal.

Her dad rinsed the dishes and loaded the dishwasher.

Trent put away the leftovers.

Mazy's dad said, "Trent. I got to hand it to you. That was the best grub I've ever eaten. I kid you not."

Earl nodded. "You out cooked my Mama. I didn't know that could be done."

Trent smiled over at Mazy. "Mazy helped out quite a bit."

She laughed. She'd made the tea and picked up the cranberry sauce from the restaurant. That's what he called "quite a bit?"

Earl asked Trent, "Have you told her?"

Trent scowled and shook his head.

Told her what? The men shared a knowing look between them. They were up to something. She could feel it in her bones.

As she plated a piece of pie for each of them and set the table, she looked out the big bay window of her breakfast nook and watched Rooster sniff around a rabbit by the creek. The little brown rabbit twitched its nose at her pig, and her pig twitched his nose right back. "Aww. Rooster's made a friend."

Trent stepped behind her and rested his hands on her hips, looking over her head out at the critters. "Well I'll be damned. Earl you got your phone on ya?"

Earl said, "Yep."

Trent said, "Come here and snap a pic before that rabbit hops off. Myrtle would love that. Ten bucks says she'll enter the picture in the weekly photography contest for the Island Gazette."

Mazy walked over to her new stainless steel refrigerator. She paused and gazed at her mother's picture on the freezer door. She spoke to her mother, silently. "Thank you, Mama.

This has been the best holiday this family's had in a long time. Family, Mama. We're a real family again. I know you had something to do with this."

Her father sat at the table first, then one by one the rest of them joined him.

The men exchanged *looks* again.

Earl said, "Come on. Can't we tell her yet?"

Trent scowled at Earl once more.

This was starting to piss her off. "Tell me what?"

Her dad shook his head. "Lord, forgive me. I can't hold it in. Your man, Trent here is thinking of buying the old skating rink and turning it into a Harley Davidson store, using the shiny wooden rink floor for the showroom. I'll let him tell you the rest."

She looked at Trent, her heart beating fast with excitement. "A Harley dealership? Holy cow. Awesome!"

Trent glared at her dad. "I'm so not telling you what I'm giving her for Christmas."

Earl laughed. "We can guess that one." He nudged his dad, and they both laughed.

Her dad smirked. "Seen that sparkly thing coming from a mile away."

Mazy could tell they were hinting at an engagement ring, or at least that's what she thought they were joking about. Little did they know, Trent had already told her he wanted to wait at least a year before taking things to the next level. It was all she could do to get him to move in with her after the house was built. He was planning on staying at the cottage until they tied the knot. Claimed he didn't want to mess anything up, wanted it to stick this time.

Trent sat his fork down. "Well, I might as well tell ya the rest, Mazy, so much for the surprise. I've been looking over the blueprints, and I think I can renovate the snack area of the rink, add on quite a bit, and build you a state of the art garage adjoining the Harley shop. That's if you want to be the top mechanic there."

She couldn't believe it. "Are you serious?"

"Yep. We can ride over and check it out later if you'd like."

"A Harley Davidson dealership. Here on the island. My very own top-notch garage. Oh. My. God!"

She jumped up and hopped into Trent's lap.

He kissed her. "Your dad's offered to call in some of his contacts to start spreading the word about the grand opening. Earl's gonna oversee the renovation, make sure all the heating and air and electrical work are done to code."

She kissed Trent again and again all over his face.

Her dad cleared his throat. "Easy there, Missy. You got an audience."

She laughed. "Y'all aren't an audience. Y'all are family!"

Earl whispered, "Amen."

Letter to Readers

Dear Reader,

I was thrilled to complete my debut novel this past December, and was completely stunned by how well it was received by so many of you. Thank you for spreading the word about my work, leaving reviews on Amazon and Goodreads, contacting me via my website, and touching base with me on Facebook and Twitter.

As I penned this book, my second novel, your words of encouragement were in my head. Also the comments concerning ways I could improve my work. I listened and tried to apply the lessons you offered about what works for you and what doesn't. I know I will never be able to please everyone, but I do strive to keep learning, and growing as an author.

I hope you have found **Rip Tide Bikini** to be as much fun as **Low Tide Bikini.** I'm working hard to establish the Lyla Dune brand as being *Hot, Hilarious, with Heart*. I feel this story hits upon those elements well, and I hope you will too.

As before, being a new author, and self published without an advertising team or big time publisher behind me, anything you can do to continue to spread the word about my work is greatly appreciated. Amazon reviews and Goodreads reviews are critical elements in the success of a book. I can't do that for myself though, so if you are so inclined to leave honest reviews, I would be forever grateful.

When I quit job to stay home and care for my ailing father, I was terrified by my loss of income, worried that I'd made the wrong decision. In my heart, I knew I wanted to be a writer. I felt that was what I was meant to do. I thought it would take several books before people took notice of my work. I can't tell you what a joy and relief it has been to see that my dream wasn't so crazy, that I was right to come home where I'm needed most, and that YES people are interested in reading my stories.

I hope to always take you to a place that is filled with laughter and love through all the ups and downs we all face in our own ways. I will strive to always leave you with a full, happy heart at the conclusion of your journey with me via my quirky characters.

Thank you so very much for your support and for taking the time to read my words. Without you, there would be no point to what I do.

Sincerely from the bottom of my heart,
Lyla Dune

P.S. Please feel free to connect with me on my website: http://www.lyladune.com
There, you will find links to subscribe to my newsletter, a contact form for direct messaging, and links to my Facebook author page and Twitter account, as well as my Pinterest account. Also, news of upcoming releases and book signings will be there, as well as any other fun things happening on the horizon for my books.

Acknowledgements

I'd like to thank my awesome critique partner, Joy Avery, who is a fabulous contemporary romance author herself. Please check out her debut novel :Smoke in the Citi.

I have two of the best beta readers ever: Whitney Belisle and Katrina Smith. These ladies really jumped in and battled my insane deadline with me. Their feedback was immensely valuable and helped to whip this book into shape.

My poor husband stayed up into the small hours, reading every word of this manuscript to me out loud as he and I searched out any stray typos. How can I help but to love a man like that?

I also called upon two young ladies from my writing group to help sort out a troublesome chapter. Mary DeSantis and Mary Loh Whitehead are two fine writers themselves. I owe them a huge thank you for assisting me with the snag I couldn't seem to unravel alone.